La signorina

e altri racconti

Texts and Translations

The Texts and Translations series was founded in 1991 to provide students and teachers with important texts not readily available or not available at an affordable price and in high-quality translations. The books in the series are intended for students in upper-level undergraduate and graduate courses in national literatures in languages other than English, comparative literature, ethnic studies, area studies, translation studies, women's studies, and gender studies. The Texts and Translations series is overseen by an editorial board composed of specialists in several national literatures and in translation studies.

Texts

1. Isabelle de Charrière. *Lettres de Mistriss Henley publiées par son amie*. Ed. Joan Hinde Stewart and Philip Stewart. 1993.
2. Françoise de Graffigny. *Lettres d'une Péruvienne*. Introd. Joan DeJean and Nancy K. Miller. 1993.
3. Claire de Duras. *Ourika*. Ed. Joan DeJean. Introd. Joan DeJean and Margaret Waller. 1994.
4. Eleonore Thon. *Adelheit von Rastenberg*. Ed. and introd. Karin A. Wurst. 1996.
5. Emilia Pardo Bazán. *"El encaje roto" y otros cuentos*. Ed. and introd. Joyce Tolliver. 1996.
6. Marie Riccoboni. *Histoire d'Ernestine*. Ed. Joan Hinde Stewart and Philip Stewart. 1998.
7. Dovid Bergelson. *Opgang*. Ed. and introd. Joseph Sherman. 1999.
8. Sofya Kovalevskaya. *Nigilistka*. Introd. Natasha Kolchevska. 2001.
9. Anna Banti. *"La signorina" e altri racconti*. Ed. and introd. Carol Lazzaro-Weis. 2001.

Translations

1. Isabelle de Charrière. *Letters of Mistress Henley Published by Her Friend*. Trans. Philip Stewart and Jean Vaché. 1993.
2. Françoise de Graffigny. *Letters from a Peruvian Woman*. Trans. David Kornacker. 1993.
3. Claire de Duras. *Ourika*. Trans. John Fowles. 1994.
4. Eleonore Thon. *Adelheit von Rastenberg*. Trans. George F. Peters. 1996.
5. Emilia Pardo Bazán. *"Torn Lace" and Other Stories*. Trans. María Cristina Urruela. 1996.
6. Marie Riccoboni. *The Story of Ernestine*. Trans. Joan Hinde Stewart and Philip Stewart. 1998.
7. Dovid Bergelson. *Descent*. Trans. Joseph Sherman. 1999.
8. Sofya Kovalevskaya. *Nihilist Girl*. Trans. Natasha Kolchevska with Mary Zirin. 2001.
9. Anna Banti. *"The Signorina" and Other Stories*. Trans. Martha King and Carol Lazzaro-Weis. 2001.

ANNA BANTI

La signorina
e altri racconti

Edited with an Introduction by
Carol Lazzaro-Weis

The Modern Language Association of America
New York 2001

Library of Congress Cataloging-in-Publication Data

Banti, Anna.
La signorina e altri racconti / Anna Banti ;
edited with an introduction by Carol Lazzaro-Weis.
p. cm. — (Texts and translations series. Texts ; 9)
Text in the original Italian with an introduction in English.
ISBN 0-87352-791-7 (pbk.)
I. Lazzaro-Weis, Carol M., 1949– II. Title. III. Texts and translations series (Modern Language Association of America). Texts ; 9.

PQ4827.O635 A6 2001
853′.912—dc21 2001042584

ISSN 1079-252X

Cover illustration of the paperback edition:
Figures in the Piazza Duomo (Three Sisters),
by Tullio Garbari (1892–1931).
Courtesy Museo di Arte Moderna e
Contemporanea di Trento e Rovereto.

Printed on recycled paper

Published by The Modern Language Association of America
26 Broadway, New York, New York 10004-1789
www.mla.org

CONTENTS

INTRODUCTION

Banti's Life and Works

Anna Banti, the literary pseudonym assumed by Lucia Lopresti-Longhi (1895–1985), is the author of eight novels, a play, seven collections of short stories, numerous critical monographs and articles, and one fictionalized version of her life and work. The recipient of prestigious literary awards; founder and coeditor with her husband of the renowned literary and art history journal *Paragone*; translator of Virginia Woolf, Colette, Alain-Fournier, and William Makepeace Thackeray, among others; and a frequent contributor to the cultural columns of Italian newspapers, the prolific Banti was a prominent figure on the Italian literary scene for almost fifty years.

Born in Florence into a family of Calabrese origin, Banti, then called Lucia Lopresti, studied art history at the University of Rome and, after a brief stint as curator of a museum in Abruzzo, married her professor Roberto Longhi, the art historian and critic. In the 1920s, several of Banti's critical essays on seventeenth-century Italian artists such as Marco Boschini, Francesco Crassia, and Francesco Cozza attracted the attention and praise of many Italian critics, including Benedetto Croce. Banti's talent for narration shone in her descriptions of the milieu and character of the artists she was studying, and, at the age of forty-two with the encouragement of her husband, Banti launched her literary career with the publication of *Itinerario di Paolina* (1937). This bildungsroman comprises loosely organized chapters that recount diverse events and experiences in the protagonist's childhood and adolescence. Although not in chronological order, they all nevertheless illustrate what would prove to be a major preoccupation of Banti's throughout her career—the representation of a female subjectivity grappling with the conflicts and solitude resulting from the desire to be different.

The language and structure of *Paolina* and Banti's other early works reflect the influence of the *prosa d'arte* movement, prominent in Italian literary circles of the 1920s and 1930s. This movement, characterized by highly stylized prose and the indirect treatment of autobiographical themes, functioned to transform reflections of the self and lived experience into descriptive pieces of poetic brilliance with broad human significance. Another influence on Banti's work was her training under Longhi, whose emphasis on formal analysis of works of art informs her elegant descriptive prose and narrative style as well as the representation of artists in her fiction. Indeed, *Artemisia* (1947), the novel that firmly established Banti's reputation as a writer, is a highly innovative blend of art history and fictionalized biography, recounting the struggle of the painter Artemisia Gentileschi, a woman attempting, like Banti herself at the time, to establish her identity as an artist.

The female artist, composer, writer, and intellectual are figures that reappear often in Banti's short stories. Banti is primarily interested, however, not in the exceptional achievements of these accomplished women but rather in their often self-destructive reactions to the isolation that they, like many women, experience. Her first two collections of short stories—*Il coraggio delle donne* (1940) and *Le monache cantano* (1942)—illustrate the bitter ironies in the struggle of women to break out of the seclusion and monotony of their daily lives. These stories of the betrayals that lead to hopelessness and social conformity are examples of Banti's second phase as an author, from the 1940s until the early 1960s, when her works were cited as examples of "realismo femminile" (Biagini 85–124). Banti also wrote three novels during this period: *Il bastardo* (1953), *Allarme sul lago* (1954), and *Le mosche d'oro* (1962). She often writes of women who feel betrayed, disparaged, or abandoned in their romantic or family relationships. Interestingly, she drew some of the plots from the *cronaca* section of newspapers, which recounts in a somewhat tabloid fashion the details of local crimes and dramas. For instance, *Il bastardo* is based on the life of a woman who, like Donna Elisa Infantado of the story, found out about the illegitimate son her husband was supporting and who may have provoked the suicide of the boy by her refusal to accept him into the family home. Whether or not they are based on actual anecdotes, the fictional works of Banti's realist period tend to represent marriage as a failed relationship and to emphasize jealousy, vengeance, and brutality as dominant experiences in the lives of many women.

In the two novels published in the late 1960s and 1970s Banti returned to fiction based not on contemporary life but on historical characters and events. The male narrator of *Noi credevamo* (1967), is based on Domenico Lopresti, a distant relative of Banti's who lived during the period of Italian unification in the nineteenth century. Her final novel, *La camicia bruciata* (1973), features the protagonist Marguerite Louise d'Orléans, who was forced by Louis XIV of France into a political marriage with an insipid husband. Banti uses a fictionalized account of the historical event to show, as she had in her earlier fiction, that exceptional talent and social position may not protect women from experiences of solitude and failure.

Although Banti's last two novels garnered major literary prizes, the headlines in the Florentine newspaper *La nazione* bidding farewell to "Artemisia" as they announced Banti's death in 1985 showed to what extent she was still identified with the heroine of the novel she had published almost forty years before. The stories in this volume have been selected to counteract the tendency to identify Banti solely with *Artemisia* and to offer a sample of the great variety to be found in her short fiction. They demonstrate that she experimented with many different genres, including fictional biography, science fiction, historical fiction, and mystery. They also show that, even as she tried various modes of representation, her interest in the plights and dilemmas of women remained constant. Indeed, the depiction of women's resistance to their disparagement and to the exclusion of their stories and themselves from the literary and social domains defined and dominated by men recurs throughout this collection, as it does in almost all her work. In "Vocazioni indistinte" (1940), Banti writes about the betrayal of women by society; in "Le donne muoiono" (1951) we see the constant denial, disruption, and silencing of women's creativity and their literary tradition; "Joveta di Betania" (1971) tells of the creative and destructive effects of enforced seclusion on women; in "I velieri" (1975) Banti portrays the stifling effects on women of bourgeois family life; and, finally, the title story, "La signorina" (1975), deals with the problems faced by a creative woman. These stories, spanning Banti's literary career, are vivid evidence of her versatility as a writer and her enduring commitment to explore in her art both the psychological and the material conditions of women.

The Personal and the Representation of Women

In interviews Banti was extremely reluctant to speak about her personal life, claiming that everything important she had to say on this topic was in her writings. Male and female critics alike have emphasized the personal element in the writing of this elusive and aloof author. Many male critics, however, tend to attribute the conflicts represented in Banti's writings to her having two incompatible careers—that of art historian and that of writer. In his preface to *Un grido lacerante*, Cesare Garboli writes that Banti's decision to become a woman writer (*una donna di lettere*) was a painful one, motivated by a need to escape the shadow of her famous professor and husband. The decision, he insists, plagued her entire literary career and informed her numerous depictions of women struggling to transgress stereotypical molds, to overcome feelings of inferiority, and to achieve the status of originators of their own art. Female critics tend to see the issue differently, interpreting Banti's use of the third person and her numerous portraits of unhappy women as evidence of a conflict between her femininity and her need to deny it in order to curry favor with the male literary establishment. For instance, speaking of Banti's "Maestra e allieva," the Italian feminist writer and critic Grazia Livi insists that for Banti "l'elemento personale [. . .] era sempre stato in qualque modo letterario e il letterario personale" (24).

Banti did not participate in feminist politics and often expressed distaste for the term. In her youth, she witnessed a number of radical transformations in Italian society, including the rise of organized feminism and socialism and the defeat of both with the coming to power of fascism in the 1920s. The Milanese activist Maria Mozzoni (1837–1920), a socialist considered to be the mother of the Italian feminist movement, believed, like Banti, that the secondary status of women had more to do with socially prescribed and limiting gender roles than with questions of class and economics. In the interest of inclusivity, however, and to get the support of the socialists, she organized the feminist movement in Italy around the question of inequality and hardship in the workplace. The initial alliance of the Italian feminist movement with a political party prefigured the secondary status of feminism on the political agenda, a status that lasted until the late 1960s, when a new generation of more radical feminists denounced the refusal of the Communist Party to separate the question of woman's status (*la questione femminile*) from the question of general economic emancipation (*la questione sociale*).

Laws passed in the first decade of the twentieth century to expand women's property rights in marriage and to protect women and children in the workplace did nothing to integrate Italian women into civic life, and private issues were not a subject of public discourse. Exceptional women, however, could live unconventional lives: Mozzoni, for instance, was a single mother, although she did not draw attention to the fact. Women's suffrage was first defeated in 1881, when universal suffrage was refused by the parliament of a recently unified Italy. In 1919, another effort to win the vote for women met defeat as the Fascists gained more power. Italian women received the vote in 1946.

Although only a few Italian women participated in civic life, during Banti's youth they were becoming highly visible as novelists and journalists. The universities had been opened officially to women in 1874, and by the turn of the century the growing number of women's journals, newspaper columns, and novels provided a forum for debate on the relation between new professions for women and women's traditional moral obligation to maintain and build a better society (Kroha 6–22). Interestingly, women's increased participation in the literary market was considered even more morally suspect than their increased presence in the blue-collar jobs usually reserved for men. Writers such as Mathilde Serao (1856–1927), Ada Negri (1870–1945), Neera (1846–1918), and Sibilla Aleramo (1876–1960) were widely read. The Sardinian writer Grazia Deledda (1871–1936) was awarded the Nobel Prize in 1926. Contemporary writers and critics who claimed to give a positive assessment of these new writers did so, however, by praising them not for their general talent but rather for what they considered the feminine aspects of their writing: a natural penchant for autobiography and a preoccupation with women's issues like marriage, divorce, abortion, and prostitution. These hallmarks were then used to explain why women's writings, mired in specific individual and topical concerns, inevitably compromised literary quality and failed to produce works of universal and long-lasting significance (Pickering-Iazzi 58–66).

Even though this response put women writers in the paradoxical position of being underestimated, as publicly prominent figures they were nevertheless under pressure to comment on women's issues. They often did so cautiously, posing as impartial observers of women's oppression by economic laws and imposed gender roles. In a more personal expression, some writers included references to their personal lives and opinions in their fictional works. For instance, Aleramo in her 1906 novel *Una donna* portrayed a character who, like her, had to abandon her son to leave an oppressive marriage. Like Neera, Serao, and Deledda, however, many women writers avoided the use of the first person and autobiographical elements in their fiction and took a public antifeminist stance.

Carolyn Heilbrun points out in *Writing a Woman's Life* that the expression of anger by women has often hindered rather than helped their personal progress. Banti renounced feminism by criticizing feminism's anger. Feminist ideology in literature was for her synonymous with the expression of an unmediated rage that threatened to divide the sexes further. She agreed with many

Italian male critics who asserted that the confessional mode associated with women's writing compromised literary quality. For instance, in a 1955 review article of Simone de Beauvoir's novel *Les mandarins*, Banti criticizes "la prima Signora dell'esistenzialismo" ("Simone de Beauvoir" 111) for the abundance of personal, confessional tendencies in the novel, which, she argues, interfere with the universal artistic and critical expression Beauvoir had demonstrated in her previous writings. Although Banti denied feminism in public discourse, she shared feminists' primary concern with sexual difference, which figures in almost all her novels and short stories. And Banti's own rage was awakened by those who insisted on classifying her according to her sex, because this category carried with it so many negative implications. Even so, she never stopped her search to find a way to define herself simultaneously as a woman and a writer.

The main conflict for women as represented in Banti's fiction is not that between two incompatible careers, as many critics have claimed, but rather between the roles that continue to be prescribed for women in literature and life. In fact, in Banti's view literature and life interact to perpetuate the disparagement of women. Portraits of women in Italian literature as either idealized projections of male desire or as evil femmes fatales motivated by perverse and uncontrollable sexual or materialist desires have perpetuated women's isolation in real life. Furthermore, the idealized or romanticized representations, according to Banti, have little to do with women's lives except to teach them to despise themselves and to degrade other women.

Banti attempted to cut through the traditional polarized views of women by writing about women's lived experience. The various forms and techniques with which she experimented enabled her to distance herself from her fiction while, at the same time, she used aspects of her experience to animate, mold, and understand the vivid characters she created. Indirectly, then, she created herself in and through her art. The "room of her own" that Banti strove to create was less a physical than a literary space where a female aesthetic could be named. To the extent that she placed herself in her fiction, a process she partially reveals in the discussions of her fictional characters in *Un grido lacerante*, she was inscribing a covert protest against the insulation of art from the actual life experiences of women. Her writings demonstrate how her identity, public and private, was linked and formed by her art in inextricable and complex ways (Lazzaro-Weis 40–42).

The Stories

It is difficult to classify Anna Banti's works. Her admitted models—Manzoni, Balzac, Dickens, and Proust—indicate that Banti was certainly influenced by various schools of realism and naturalism as well as by the psychological novel. As a chronicler of women, she is also linked in many ways to works of the women writers she translated, namely, Woolf, Austen, and Colette. Unlike some of her models, though, Banti is not interested in portraying her characters as products of psychological or socially determined forces. Her work is grounded in specific situations, highlighting the reactions and sometimes incongruous behavior of her protagonists after they have suffered a real or perceived injustice, most often related to their status as a woman. Although influenced by the male-dominated *prosa d'arte* movement, Banti's crafted and often dense prose is tinged with an irony emerging from the incongruity between the lofty dreams and aspirations of her female characters and the defeat ultimately awaiting them.

"Vocazioni indistinte," which first appeared in 1940, was republished in two short story collections: *"La monaca di Sciangai" e altri racconti* (1957) and *Campi Elisi* (1963). All the stories in these collections detail in some way the dull, repetitive nature of women's lives where real heroism and accomplishment are lacking. Women of varying talents in Banti's fiction avail themselves of three means of establishing their identity: study, work, and artistic creation. Since, however, the world of self-satisfying work is one that women have been taught to avoid by finding the right male mediator-savior, these solutions meet with, at best, limited degrees of success.

Work is the solution attempted by the protagonist of "Vocazioni indistinte," who is an average petite bourgeoise. Ofelia's character is replete with increasingly grotesque pathological complexes as she desperately tries to define and redefine herself when her goals are changed for her by chance and family circumstance. Ofelia oscillates between two supposedly antithetical vocations, that of wife and mother and that of independent woman. At the beginning of the story, her main accomplishments in life are surviving typhus and managing to pass her exams with diligent study. Her family hopes that these successes will enable her to get a husband. However, the secure life of a married woman appears out of reach when a courtship falls through and

Ofelia is required to choose the second vocation, that of the independent, self-sufficient women described in the women's journals of the time. By dint of hard work she manages to become a piano teacher of some repute before she resorts to marriage to escape endless self-doubts and a worsened family situation.

The predominance of indirect discourse and irony in the story links Banti's Ofelia to Flaubert's naive, hard-working maid Félicité in his short story "Un cœur simple" (1877; "A Simple Heart"). After a series of rejections, the faulty reasoning of both women colludes with society's unfair treatment of them to ensure that they will not prosper. The basic literary structure here is that of a negative fairy tale: Ofelia's search for autonomy through work is perceived by her as well as by others as a punishment for her lack of success in attracting a man. Rarely comfortable with her profession, the working woman is an outsider in the circles she frequents. Ofelia receives some support for her talent from her more attractive and self-confident cousin Giulia. All portraits are tinged with parodic irony, however. Banti exposes the hypocrisy of the middle class; the insincere, self-aggrandizing attitudes toward art of the Italian intelligentsia; and the cliché-ridden opinions of Giulia and her female friends. Female solidarity is a short-lived dream, and Ofelia's career is viewed by both Ofelia and her family as another way to make her attractive. In the final scene of this domestic fairy tale gone awry, Giulia visits an impoverished Ofelia held captive by her prince and her children. Like her Shakespearean namesake, Ofelia seems to have gone insane, a victim of the dream that women can escape a subservient destiny with a job or a dowry.

Very different from "Vocazioni indistinte," "Le donne muoiono" is one of three science fiction stories by Banti. Published with three other short stories composed between 1938 and 1950 in a collection of the same name, "Le donne muoiono" received the prestigious Viareggio Prize in 1952. Using the science fiction genre to speculate about the innate differences between men and women, Banti imagines the utopian and dystopian possibilities of a world that is biologically defined. As in her historical works, the science fiction narrative depicts the permanence of male control over history and female destiny.

Published two years after Simone de Beauvoir's novel *Tous les hommes sont mortels* (1947; "All Men Are Mortal"), "Le donne muoiono" shares many of its themes. Both women writers show how men's desire for immortality can cause men to lose their humanity at the same time that it motivates heroic actions, foolish or otherwise. While Beauvoir's book is situated within a debate about existential philosophy, Banti's story, a parody of Fascism's attempts to revive Italy's glorious past, emphasizes how men's desire for immortality excludes women. "Le donne muoiono" also bears a strong resemblance to Margaret Atwood's more recent dystopian science fiction novel *A Handmaid's Tale* (1987), since both depict the return of women's oppression after a period of supposed progress and emancipation. Banti's Agnese would agree with Atwood's handmaid narrator that it is men who possess time whereas women only endure it.

Set in the year 2617, "Le donne muoiono" depicts the return of women's oppression when sexual difference again becomes a means of isolating and disparaging women. Science has made progress in areas such as hygiene and rational education, and men and women enjoy equality in the public domain. However, this situation changes when men discover that they can remember past lives. This "seconda memoria" allows them to conquer their traditional fear of death and to claim immortality for themselves through constant reincarnation. Unable to participate in this self-preserving and self-serving continuum, many women retreat to female communities, which resemble the convents of old, to lament their fate among themselves.

Atwood's handmaids are child-bearing machines for select white males whose resentful but cooperating wives can no longer give them children. Women either support this system or are deported. In "Le donne muoiono" women again become procreation machines and their own worst enemies. Real love between the sexes is impossible, since the point of any sexual union is to have sons. Even Banti's dream of parity in the literary world is reversed as women's search for identity through creation leads to the same effacement as before. Liberated from domestic duties, women are free to create and even dominate the realm of literature. But their masterpieces are ignored by the male establishment, which has marginalized all practitioners of the arts because they produce works that are overwhelmingly "triste" and lacking in heroism. Banti's dislike for the ideological realism in literature espoused by contemporary writers and critics is revealed in her remark that men assumed that literature was dead and that a new poetry would take place only when the new society (brought about by the endless reincarnations of males) was realized. The female communities testify not to female creative ability but to women's ultimate impotence, since they make women's isolation and solitude a permanent state of being.

In this volume's third story, a religious community takes the place of the female communities in "Le donne muoiono." The portrayal of women's entrapment and marginalization is less parodic. "Joveta di Betania," which centers on an abbess in eleventh-century Antioch, first appeared in a collection of short stories with a French title, *Je vous écris d'un pays lointain* (1971). "Joveta" counteracts some of the more negative images of sequestered women found in Banti's works of the 1950s and 1960s. Obliged to become a nun after attempts at arranged marriages fail, Joveta is increasingly committed to learning and independence, but in a way that is stronger, though only slightly, than Ofelia's. The passionate Joveta is wounded by a man's rejection (imagined) and by the inability of her family to find her a suitable marriage partner. Her choice will be to study, and the convent financed by her sister will be a place of learning and security, much like a "harem senza letto coniugale." Joveta becomes a distinguished abbess and founder of a community that encourages the intellectual and aesthetic capacities of women. Even though, like her creator Banti, Joveta has no desire to be a mother, she joyfully serves as a mentor to her beloved niece, Melisenda, who is placed for safety in Joveta's care until a marriage partner can be found for her. The failure of the arranged marriage of Melisenda due to political rivalries will destroy her life. It will also destroy Joveta's intellectual legacy, since at the end Joveta, like Ofelia, is represented as falling into an embittered and seemingly senile state as she awaits death.

The final two stories of this volume appeared in Banti's last published short story collection, *Da un paese vicino* (1975). The title of the collection underlines that these narratives are contemporary, in contrast to the predominantly historical fiction of the previous collection. In "I velieri," the main character is Jean, a young Swiss boy. The surprise ending overturns all expectations created by his efforts to protest against his monotone existence as a rich industrialist's son. What is perhaps more interesting is Banti's shift to a male protagonist. But the shift is only apparent: the disappointments and delusions previously described as being part of women's search for adventure and a meaningful existence inform Banti's depiction of the dreams and aspirations of the sequestered boy, who is as powerless and isolated as the women portrayed earlier. The mother in the story, who is reminiscent of Virginia Woolf's Mrs. Flanders in *Jacob's Room*, is also an ambivalent figure: while she is overprotective toward her son, she is, like many other female characters in Banti, defeated in her attempts to show and share love.

"La signorina" is a thinly disguised self-portrait of the young Banti's struggle with her own "vocazioni indistinte" as a woman searches to define herself as a woman writer. The main character in the story confronts two traditional female destinies, the young or old maid indicated by the title (*la signorina*) and the married woman (*la signora*), as she evolves from one into the other. Despite differences in class and intelligence, the signorina is no different from Banti's other protagonists in her desire for recognition, independence, and love. Fluctuating between the ironic and the tragic, the older woman reflects on her former self in ways that connect her to both Ofelia and Joveta. In this story, however, instead of disappearing into a state of mental or physical decrepitude, the divided self forgives the woman's choice to love and marry and accepts the price, however high, that she has to pay.

In *Un grido lacerante*, the final compendium of Banti and all her fictional heroines, the narrator, Agnese, bids an emotional farewell to her professor-husband in a dream in which they both agree that "la vera vita era quella dell'opera d'arte" (*Un grido lacerante* 174). This androgynous vision of art identifies Banti as one of the generation of women who sought to maintain their femininity while integrating it in a world that men still dominated. That this endeavor is unending means that Banti's works and life continue to speak to us in the present. Although immortality is reserved for the creative space men and women share, they share this space by displaying the differences Banti never denied and spent her life illuminating in explicit detail. Her commitment to exploring the question of sexual difference links her work to women writing now. And her novels and short stories stand together as a protest against those times that ever threaten to recur, when the fact that a work of art was written by a woman was sufficient reason to ignore it.

Works Cited and Consulted

Banti, Anna. "Ermengarda e Geltrude." *Paragone* 52 (1954): 23–30.

———. *Un grido laceranto*. Milan: Rizzoli, 1981.

———. "Simone de Beauvoir." *Paragone* 64 (1955): 110–12.

Ballaro, Beverly. "Anna Banti (Lucia Lopresti Longhi), 1895–1985." *Italian Women Writers: A Bio-bibliographical Sourcebook*. Ed. Rinaldina Russell. Westport: Greenwood, 1994. 35–43.

Biagini, Enza. *Anna Banti*. Milan: Mursia, 1978.

Blelloch, Paola. "Anna Banti da 'Il coraggio delle donne' a 'Le donne muoiono.'" *NEMLA Italian Studies* 11 (1987–88): 97–104.

Gallucci, Carole. "Anna Banti: On the Courage of Women." *Colophon* 4 (1988): 69–76.

Garboli, Cesare. Preface. Banti, *Un grido* 1–3.

Garrard, Mary. *Artemisia Gentileschi: The Image of the Female Hero in Italian Baroque Art*. Princeton: Princeton UP, 1989.

Greer, Germaine. *The Obstacle Race: The Fortunes of Women Painters and Their Work*. New York: Farrar, 1979.

Heilbrun, Carolyn. *Writing a Woman's Life*. New York: Ballantine, 1988.

Kroha, Lucienne. *The Woman Writer in Late Nineteenth-Century Italy: Gender and the Formation of Literary Identity*. Lewiston: Mellen, 1992.

Lazzaro-Weis, Carol. "Stranger than Life: Autobiography and Historical Fiction." *Gendering Italian Fiction: Feminist Revisions of Italian History*. Ed. Maria Ornella Marotti and Gabriella Brooke. Madison: Fairleigh Dickinson UP, 1999. 31–48.

Lefanu, Sarah. *In the Chinks of the World Machine: Feminism and Science Fiction*. London: Women's, 1988.

Lerner, Gerda. *The Creation of a Feminist Consciousness: From the Middle Ages to Eighteen-Seventy*. Oxford: Oxford UP, 1993.

Livi, Grazia. "Maestra e allieva." *Racconta*. Milan: La Tartaruga, 1989. 17–25.

Meyer, Donald, *Sex and Power: The Rise of Women in America, Russia, Sweden, and Italy*. Middletown: Wesleyan UP, 1987.

Petrignani, Sandra. *Le signore della scrittura*. Milan: La Tartaruga, 1984.

Pickering-Iazzi, Robin. *Politics of the Invisible: Writing Women, Culture, and Fascism*. Minneapolis: U of Minnesota P, 1997.

Valentini, Daria. "Anna and Her Sisters: The Idyll of the Convent in Anna Banti." *Forum italicum* 30.2 (1996): 132–350.

BIBLIOGRAPHY

Works by Anna Banti

MAJOR NOVELS

Itinerario di Paolina. Rome: Augustea, 1937.

Sette lune. Milan: Bompiani, 1941.

Artemisia. Florence: Sansoni, 1947. Milan: Mondadori, 1953, 1969. Milan: Oscar, 1974.

Il bastardo. Florence: Sansoni, 1953. Milan: Mondadori, 1961 (as *La casa piccola*).

Allarme sul lago. Milan: Mondadori, 1954.

Le mosche d'oro. Milan: Mondadori, 1962.

Noi credevamo. Milan: Mondadori, 1967, 1969 (in *Due storie*).

La camicia bruciata. Milan: Mondadori, 1973.

Un grido lacerante. Milan: Rizzoli, 1981.

SHORT STORY COLLECTIONS

Il coraggio delle donne. Florence: Le Monnier, 1940.

Le monache cantano. Rome: Tuminelli, 1942.

Le donne muoiono. Milan: Mondadori, 1951.

"La monaca di Sciangai" e altri racconti. Milan: Mondadori, 1957.

Campi Elisi. Milan: Mondadori, 1963.

Je vous écris d'un pays lointain. Milan: Mondadori, 1971.

Da un paese vicino. Milan: Mondadori, 1975.

SELECTED CRITICAL WORKS

Lorenzo Lotto. Florence: Sansoni, 1953.

Fra Angelico. Milan: Garzanti, 1953.

Diego Velázquez. Milan: Garzanti, 1955.

Claude Monet. Milan: Garzanti, 1956.

Opinioni. Milan: Il Saggiatore, 1961.

Matilde Serao. Turin: UTET, 1965.

Giovanni da San Giovanni: Pittore della contraddizione. Florence: Sansoni, 1977.

Quando anche le donne si misero a dipingere. Milan: Tartaruga, 1982.

TRANSLATIONS

William Makepeace Thackeray, *La fiera delle vanità*. Milan: Longanesi, 1948.

Virginia Woolf, *La camera di Jacob*. Milan: Mondadori, 1950.

Francis Carco, *L'amico dei pittori*. Milan: Martello, 1955.

André Chastel, *L'arte italiana*. Florence: Sansoni, 1957–58.

Alain-Fournier, *Il gran Meaulnes*. Milan: Mondadori, 1974. Preface by Banti.

Colette, *La vagabonda*. Milan: Mondadori, 1977. Preface by Banti.

Works by Anna Banti in English Translation

NOVELS

Artemisia. Trans. Shirley D'Ardia Caracciolo. Lincoln: U of Nebraska P, 1988.

A Piercing Cry [*Un grido lacerante*]. Trans. Daria Valentini and S. Mark Lewis. New York: Lang, 1996.

SHORT STORIES

"The Courage of Women" ["Il coraggio delle donne"]. Trans. Martha King. *New Italian Women: A Collection of Short Fiction*. New York: Italica, 1989. 1–22.

"The Truth about Beatrice" ["Verità su Beatrice"]. Trans. Paola Carù. *Forum italicum* 32.1 (1998): 210–14.

"Laura's Pleasures" ["Piaceri di Laura"]. Trans. Paola Carù. *Forum italicum* 32.1 (1998): 215–18.

Selected Criticism

Belotti, Elena. "Anna Banti e il femminismo." Biagini, *L'opera* 111–18.

Biagini, Enza, ed. *L'opera di Anna Banti: Convegno di studi*. Florence: Olschi, 1997.

———. "La poesia e la filosofia della storia : Anna Banti e Marguerite Yourcenar." Biagini, *L'opera* 93–106.

Cannon, JoAnn. "Artemisia and the Life Story of the Exceptional Woman." *Forum italicum* 28.2 (1994): 322–39.

Finucci, Valeria. "Anna Banti." *An Encyclopedia of Continental Women Writers*. Vol. 1. Ed. Katharina M. Wilson. New York: Garland, 1991.

Guerriccho, Rita. "Vite vere e immaginarie di Anna Banti." Biagini, *L'opera* 71–86.

Nozzoli, Anna. "Anna Banti: La scelta del romanzo storico." *Tabù e coscienza: La condizione femminile nella letteratura italiana del Novecento*. Florence: La Nuova Italia, 1978. 85–111.

Papini, Maria Carla. "Artemesia e Orlando." Biagini, *L'opera* 119–34.

Valentini, Daria. "A House of Mirrors: Cases of Spatial Disintegration in Anna Banti's Fiction." *Romance Languages Annual* 7 (1995): 350–56.

Volpi, Marisa. "*Un grido lacerante*: Idealizzazione e verità." Biagini, *L'opera* 191–97.

Wood, Sharon. *Italian Women's Writing, 1860–1994*. London: Athlone, 1995. 119–34.

NOTE ON EDITIONS

Many of Anna Banti's short narrative pieces appeared in periodicals and newspapers during the 1930s and 1940s. Her "racconti lunghi" translated here appeared in short story collections with the exception of "Le donne muoiono," which was first published in the literary journal *Botteghe oscure* in 1950 and then appeared in the short story collection of the same name by Mondadori in 1951. In the 1951 edition, Banti gives the date of composition as 1938. When the story was republished in *Campi Elisi* (1963), she changed the date to 1940. "Vocazioni indistinte" was written in 1938 and published in *Il coraggio delle donne* (1940). Both these works appeared again in *La monaca di Sciangai e altri racconti* (1957) and *Campi Elisi* (1963). "Joveta di Betania" first appeared in *Je vous écris d'un pays lointain*, by Mondadori in 1971, and was never republished. The same is true for "I velieri" and "La signorina," both of which first appeared in *Da un paese vicino* in 1975.

That these stories were published in collections did not make them easier to obtain, since the volumes went rapidly out of print. The feminist publishing house La Tartaruga published "Vocazioni indistinte" and "Le donne muoiono" along with three other stories in 1983 in another collection entitled *Il coraggio delle donne*, although this edition is now out of print. In 1998, "Le donne muoiono" and three other short stories edited by Grazia Livi were published in a collection of the same name (by Giunti in Florence).

In this volume, the following editions were used:

"Vocazioni indistinte." *Il coraggio delle donne*. Milan: La Tartaruga, 1983

"Le donne muoiono." *Il coraggio delle donne*. Milan: La Tartaruga, 1983

"Joveta di Betania." *Je vous écris d'un pays lointain*. Milan: Mondadori, 1971

"La signorina." *Da un paese vicino*. Milan: Mondadori, 1975

"Il velieri." *Da un paese vicino*. Milan: Mondadori, 1975

ANNA BANTI

La signorina
e altri racconti

VOCAZIONI INDISTINTE

Passato il tifo, l'Ofelia fu promossa, in città e in casa, a bella ragazza. Le erano spuntati sul capo certi riccioloni opachi che guarnivano un viso di topo, prima malamente stirato alle tempie dall'urgenza delle treccioline strette. Per le guance le si andava diffondendo una floridezza molliccia che, se accentuava la patatina del naso, nell'insieme alleggeriva i contorni e non poteva dispiacere. Il corpo non prometteva gran che, ma l'andatura puerile di prima, a passetti precipitosi di scolara zelante, aveva dato luogo a una lentezza trasandata che evocava, senza proporle, le grazie di una altezza eccessiva, in attesa di suggerire più tardi il languore di una donna affaticata dai troppi parti. In città si diceva che il dottore suo padre stesse accumulando certe leggendarie economie per farle una gran dote: sicché arrivò il momento che la sua fama crebbe, come avviene in provincia, smisuratamente; e l'Ofelia fu quasi di moda.

Era essa stata, fino allora, una ragazzetta arida, egualmente negata al buon senso e alla fantasia. Cresciuta in una casa che la madre teneva con un regime pedante di disordine e di avarizia, aveva, fin da piccola, condannato, esecrato quei metodi; disordinata e pedante essa stessa, come per maledizione. Considerate le sue scarse qualità mentali, cui suppliva peraltro un accanimento diligente e come uno sperpero di buona volontà, l'avevano mandata, dopo le elementari, alle scuole tecniche, e intanto vagamente avviata allo studio del piano. Queste risoluzioni tradivano due ragionamenti consecutivi e contraddittori, tipici di certe famiglie borghesi. « Non ha fantasia, dunque avviamola alla pratica; non ama le scienze, e allora dovrebbe riuscire nell'arte ». Così la fanciulla aveva patito il doppio martirio di lavorare in due campi diversi colla stessa fatica e il medesimo contraggenio. Eran forse queste amarezze che avevan favorito in lei una permalosità eccessiva, più efficace di una frusta a spingerla ai maggiori sforzi. I parenti poterono finalmente annunciare successi ottenuti a prezzo di sangue, ed esclamare: « Quanto amor proprio »: che sugli ultimi dell'ottocento era elogio prediletto dagli educatori e valeva un oroscopo felice. Invece la ragazzina agiva per una immane paura di non si sa quali disprezzi e beffeggi che sul suo conto le parevan sempre imminenti, e ai quali non poteva pensare senza perdere la testa. Era anche molto invidiosa, ma umilmente, in tono di rassegnazione melanconica, senza slancio né intensità; smaltendo in silenzio i livori che le cauterizzavano il cuore e lo rendevano, via via, più duro e chiuso. Un egoismo cruccioso, male affidato al sostegno di un carattere debolissimo e senza fiducia di sé: ecco il resultato di sedici anni di vita. Stupiva, in tal clima, quella tenacia, quella inclinazione allo sforzo disperato che prosperava, nel suo corpicciolo, come le vecce in cantina.

Figuriamoci quest'essere, tuttora adolescente, uscir fievole fievole da una gran malattia e respirare per la prima volta un'aria melliflua, anzi, addirittura eccitante, di complimenti e di adulazioni. Per l'appunto la malattia era durata tutta un'estate e aveva distrutto il raccapriccio delle fatiche scolastiche, quell'anno gravissime in occasione degli esami di licenza. Ora, col freschetto dell'autunno e il torpore del benessere, il diploma sospirato le pareva piovuto dal cielo e ottenuto colla facilità delle sue compagne più furbe e ricche di stratagemmi. I parenti, per la contentezza della guarigione e per la compiacenza del felice sviluppo fisico, le facevan festa come mai: da quella figliola sghemba era uscita all'improvviso una ragazza corteggiabile, maritabilissima. Che fortuna. Alle congratulazioni dei conoscenti la madre rispondeva con la faccia di una donna che sa il fatto suo e ha preparato sottomano un bel gioco; né cambiava espressione o mostrava d'infastidirsi se, per l'ingordigia degli indiscreti provinciali, il discorso passava dalle qualità della figlia ad aperti scandagli sul suo appannaggio dotale. Con un sorrisetto stitico e un ammiccare degli occhi lippi, pensava di tenerli tutti a bada, mentre, ruminando piani cervellotici, non s'accorgeva che avvalorare i sospetti di ricchezze nascoste, poteva essere una tattica pericolosa.

L'autunno trascorreva placido, ma di scuole per l'Ofelia non si parlava. Eppure essa ricordava benissimo le discussioni famigliari, percepite attraverso la pauraccia degli esami e i primi brividi del tifo: istituto tecnico, passaggio alle normali, ammissione al conservatorio. Per lei eran tutti propositi egualmente feroci che però, nella crisi del momento, non la spaventavano neanche, sicura com'era che un bel giorno non ce l'avrebbe fatta più e sarebbe cascata a sedere. Nei suoi ozi, ora, a letto o in poltrona, col ricamino cincischiato fra le mani, qualche passo di quei discorsi le riecheggiava in mente. « Una donna deve bastare a sé stessa ». « Gli studi commerciali sono più moderni, aprono mille strade ». « L'insegnamento del piano è una professione più gentile ». Come nuvolacce queste sentenze di malaugurio s'eran disciolte nel sereno attuale. « Troppo bello » pensava l'Ofelia, e trascurava di respirare a pieni polmoni per guardarsi intorno, sospettosa. Dov'era l'agguato? A momenti la sua pedantissima credulità giungeva ad allarmarla nei riguardi del suo avvenire, e proprio nel senso che fino allora le era sembrato nemico. Dunque nessuno pensava più a lei; se non si fosse maritata l'avrebbero lasciata morir di fame. Altre volte le sue abitudini di diffidenza e di pessimismo le avvelenavano piaceri inusitati: l'offerta di un cappellino, di un gingillo, la prova di un nuovo vestito. Come mai tanta prodigalità, cosa c'era sotto? Così almanaccando, perdeva la gioia di queste dolcezze che, più tardi, nella luce dei confronti, non conservarono neanche il fascino dei buoni ricordi.

Piano piano, tuttavia, trascorso il mese d'ottobre, la ragazza fu certa di esser stata messa, sensa avviso, su nuove rotaie. Colle prime passeggiate e le prime visite la coscienza di aver subíto una felice metamorfosi non le mancò, ma la sua natura esigente e scontenta non le permise di goderne per intero. Innanzi, tutto, ragionando, le pareva una grossa ingiustizia il dover la bellezza a una malattia mortale. « Grazie tante, e se ci rimanevo? » Poi lo specchio rivelando a una a una le piccole magagne del viso, il sentimento della fanciulla era quello di chi si accorge d'aver pagata troppo cara una mercanzia sospetta. « Tutto qui? » pareva significare in quegli istanti la smorfia della sua bocca minuta; e nondimeno il volto toccatole in sorte le cominciò a divenire carissimo. Lo difendeva accanitamente contro chiunque tentasse per ischerzo sminuirne i pregi o sembrasse, vantandone un altro, opporgli un contraltare nocivo. Così può esser protetto il tesoro della vedova. In quei giorni i parenti si compiacevano a raccontare in confidenza come, avendole sporta un giovanetto una lettera amorosa, Ofelia la consegnasse al padre, credendola diretta a lui. « Che ingenuità » era il commento atteso, ma non sarebbe stato difficile spiegar quel tratto con un accesso acuto di almanaccante distrazione, impermeabile a ogni spontaneo riflesso.

Coll'inverno le forze ritornarono, e fu deciso che l'Ofelia si rimettesse al piano. Dalla convalescenza le era rimasta l'abitudine, non contrastata, di levarsi tardi, sicché non entrava mai in salotto prima delle undici. Chiusa la porta, essa rimaneva un momento ferma e come indecisa, in quell'ombriccia formentata di canfora che è di regola, in provincia, nelle stanze di ricevimento. In un angolo il vecchio piano lustrava dalla coda come un biscione, e la ragazza sbadigliando e ancheggiando stracca al suo nuovo modo, s'avviava e alzava il coperchio della tastiera. Ora la madre non l'assillava più col controllo del tempo impiegato negli esercizi e coll'imposizione del terribile metronomo. Le aveva procurato anzi, degli spartiti d'opere, e aveva pregata la maestra di alleggerire la lezione, « perché la ragazza era ancora debolina ». Succedeva che di tutta quella libertà e indulgenza l'Ofelia non sapeva che fare; ormai, in fatto di occupazione, solo il lavoro duro e ansioso, il compito ingrato le erano comprensibili, e trovarsi così, senza briglia, abbandonata al proprio piacere, le dava noia. E poi, qual'era il suo piacere?

Messe le dita sui tasti, cominciava macchinalmente uno dei vecchi esercizi, a casaccio. I suoni e le loro combinazioni non le davano nessun gusto e anche l'orecchio li rifiutava; mancava l'impegno di superare una difficoltà in un tempo breve e determinato dall'incalzare di altri assilli, dunque veniva a sparire l'interesse e quell'alternarsi di scrupoli e di superstiziosi patti del diavolo (arrivare alla settima battuta senza errori, riuscire alla terza ripetizione di un passo d'agilità) da cui la sua natura rimaneva attratta. Se fra uno studio e l'altro indugiava un poco, immobile a testa bassa sugli avori, non era per trattenere intime risonanze o per gustare il silenzio, il profumo vecchiotto della sala, ma per una svagatezza smorta, ronzante da lontano di meschini appelli: recriminazioni del giorno innanzi, dispettucci subiti, tutto l'armamentario di cui in pochi mesi era venuta munendo la sua posizione di ragazza da marito. Gli avvilimenti della sgobbona pusillanime rinascevano nelle gare quotidiane per il ricciolo più serrato o la vita più sottile. Soltanto che, maldestra, l'Ofelia non sapeva da che parte incominciare per ottenere la solite sanguinose vittorie; e per questo, esagerando i vezzi altrui e le proprie irrimediabili mancanze, continuava a rodersi.

Né si creda che i complimenti a cui seguitava a venir fatta segno, la incoraggiassero e consolassero. Subito ci s'era abituata come a un tributo che faceva parte del nuovo stato, una specie di media di sufficienza che guai fosse venuta a mancare; sicché anche per il costante e inutile lavorío della mente, non li registrava, avessero pur la voce di giovani schietti, in cui il suo istinto avrebbe dovuto ravvisare aspiranti probabili. Senza riflettere ai mezzi pratici di trovare un marito buono, attendeva a rimuginare sui propri requisiti fisici, morali, pecuniari, tutti in un mazzo, e valutarli come titoli freddi, sottoposti all'eterna bilancia dei confronti, della richiesta e dell'offerta: né le veniva in mente che esistessero in questo campo squilibri o modi semplici di farli salire e di imporli. Tanto valeva oggi il suo viso, tanto doveva valere, né più né meno: a chi le avesse presentato un gran partito, rispondente, secondo lei, ai più alti gradi del merito femminile, avrebbe fatto spallucce d'incredulità e persino di fastidio, più che mai sentendo il bisogno, in questa materia fallace, di appoggiare le spalle a qualcosa come un ordine sicuro e sanzionato. Da qualche tempo, piuttosto, il suo cervello s'invischiava nella abitudine di fare i conti sulle facoltà della famiglia e sui propri diritti in vista di un collocamento. La tenuta, la villa di Poppi, le case di San Lino: ingenue cifre, tratte da frammentarie induzioni, formicolavano sciogliendosi in sospettosi interrogativi e sconfortanti pessimismi. Già si sa, la parte più grossa, le terre che rendono, andranno a Giorgio. Ieri stesso la mamma difendeva il Cocchi che lasciò tutto al maschio e alla figliola soltanto una magra legittima. « È così senz'altro, anche a me daranno la legittima ». E le famose economie e i diamanti della nonna? Altri computi, altri benefici da contendere, da rimpiangere già. Con quegli occhi rotondi troppo distanti dal piccolo naso, ma spalancati e fissi, l'Ofelia ricordava l'aspetto di un uccello avido stupido e paziente. In fondo all'animo suo speranze e timori venivano accuratamente archiviati, in silenzio. Qualche volta si sfogava, è vero, colle serve, colla cucitrice a giornata o, in villa, con una contadina di mezza età, mammana delle massaie dei dintorni: tutte persone umili, a cui umilmente ella esponeva lunghe querimonie distribuite in racconti ricchissimi di dettagli, di induzioni, di dubbi. L'antica permalosità rifioriva: « ha detto così e così, ha fatto il tal gesto, ha voluto far capire quest'altro ». Il suo piccolo mondo diventava un bosco pieno di trappole. Quelle donne, prima curiose, poi annoiate, o la dissuadevano con ossequio ma senza interesse o fingevano di adottare il suo punto di vista e le sue ragioni con equivoco calore. Del resto essa neppur le ascoltava, saziata di poter andare avanti, a voce alta colle supposizioni e i sospetti. Così il tempo, senza risultati visibili, passava.

Il bello fu quando, trascorso un paio d'anni, fu scoperto in famiglia che la ragazza faceva all'amore di nascosto. Una vecchia zia vedova, tenuta in casa con sopportazione, utile quando poteva, ma ormai cieca e sorda per prudenza ed esperienza, si lasciò scappar di bocca che se n'era accorta da un pezzo. « Come, come » gridava la madre « e io che ci sto a fare? Perché non avvisarmi subito? Il cuore di una mamma... ». Seguitò un pezzo a lamentarsi, piacendole molto discorrer sensibile e forbito, e tutti tacevano, con gli altri la incriminata. Poi si calmò, e anzi il suo atteggiamento verso la figlia fu soccorrevole tanto da far sospettare una vecchia e muta complicità. Pure l'innamorato non era gran cosa, uno studentino, nipote di un canonico venuto di fuori; e non si capiva come la signora Ernesta, con tutte le sue pretese, se ne accontentasse, giacché non era tipo da cedere al sentimento. La spiegazione poteva forse ritrovarsi nell'interesse e nel rispetto che in certe donne anziane e tardi maritate, germoglia per le vicende amorose delle proprie figliole di giovanissima età. Quel miraggio di aver sottomano una sposa diciottenne, del proprio sangue, e poterne controllare i moti coi diritti materni, riesce talvolta una molla infallibile. In ogni caso nessuno avrebbe negato che non fosse questo il primo passo dell'Ofelia sulla strado del matrimonio, anche se un poco sbandato e incerto. La signora Ernesta parve messa di buon umore, celiava con altera futilità e riceveva il ragazzo in casa con garbo un po' distratto, e a titolo di semplice amicizia, sicché non era raro che l'Ofelia rimanesse sola con lui, in salotto. La vecchia zia si scandalizzava fra sé, ma aveva torto perché la ragazza non poteva ispirar colpi di testa. Come avesse fatto, piuttosto, a imbastire un amoretto romantico, lei così lontana dai gusti e dai pensieri che lo favoriscono, non fu mai chiaro. Forse agiva, incontrollata, la gentilezza dell'età; o il capriccio del giovane, nato dalla sopravvalutazione cittadina della fanciulla, funzionò da calamita. Questa volta il biglietto d'amore fu trattenuto e con una contentezza gelosa: l'assillata creatura si guardò intorno, riconobbe l'innamorato, le parve una cosa straordinaria, quell'oggettivarsi improvviso d'un fenomeno necessario e distante fino allora come una disciplina di scuola. Meraviglia e soddisfazione facilitarono l'opera della natura, sicché, timidamente, anche la povera gallinella s'innamorava.

Ma, in quell'episodio, i momenti di autentica freschezza furono pochi. Mentre la madre andava in giro con un'arietta misteriosa e gonfia — si sa, le ragazze vistose attirano i mosconi — Ofelia inacidiva e corrompeva la gioia del suo cuore colle solite argomentazioni e induzioni terra terra. La famiglia chiudeva un occhio, dunque non le riconosceva possibilità d'altri candidati. Il romantico corteggiatore si chiuse nei contorni del promesso, del sicuro marito. Così si sarebbe collocata, quella era l'occasione che una sua pari poteva pretendere, non c'era da aspettare altro. In tal modo la giovane trascurava di baloccarsi col nuovo sentimento o, su un piede più intimo, di compiacersi nella sicurezza d'aver fatto una scelta, di voler bene, ch'era pur la verità dell'animo suo. Come uno che ha investito mediocremente un capitaletto e già un po' scontento fa i conti sulla magra rendita, essa si perdeva a fantasticare su un avvenire tutto restrizioni e umiltà: una umiltà che, come sempre, non la pacificava, ma, ai suoi occhi, giustificava quel vano lavorar di trivello nel tronco del proprio futuro. Addizioni stentate, problematiche, già corrose dal pessimismo in ogni capo; dubbi sulla futura posizione di Rinaldo, sugli aiuti dello zio prete, perfino sulla esistenza del podere nel Canavese di cui il ragazzo, per altro, non vantava che i fiordalisi nel grano.

Fra le consolazioni intere dell'Ofelia può contarsi, in quei giorni lo sguardo stupito di una bimbetta undicenne, ospite autunnale di casa sua: figlia di un parente professionista, agiato, ma senza beni solidi, e dunque considerato povero in paese. Quello sguardo limpido e assorto non finiva di divagare intorno alla segreta scoperta che le cugina « grande » avesse un innamorato, e qualunque ragazza ci avrebbe riso sopra. Non così l'Ofelia che anzi sentiva di ricevere un omaggio e una conferma alle sue vitali teorie di classificazione umana: credendo a un moto di desiderio, di invidia, perché, secondo lei, a quella ragazzetta senza dote non sarebbe toccato, a suo tempo, nemmeno un Rinaldo. Il supposto sentimento le pareva giusto e quasi doveroso come i suoi propri verso altre fanciulle meglio fornite; l'avessero disingannata ne avrebbe patito come per una ingiustizia. Un altro effetto della sua conquista, fu l'attutirsi di quell'aspro bisogno di fatica che gli anni di scuola le avevan lasciato insoddisfatto. Giudicandosi ormai al riparo da certe inquietudini, cominciò a manifestare una pietà quasi schifiltosa per le donne destinate a procacciarsi da vivere col lavoro personale. « Poverina » ripeteva tutte le volte che si nominava la cuginetta, « si capisce, non ha dote, deve studiare, affaticarsi per arrivare a una posizione ». La voce era arida, monotona, il cervello andava a zonzo in cerca di egoistiche quisquilie, ma le parole parevan contate e suggerite da un obbligo tradizionale e imparate a mente. Poi, la bambina ritornata a Roma, il piacere di immaginarsi invidiata divenne ben raro; al solito per sfogarsi e sentirsi a posto non le rimase che rivolgersi alle serve di casa; qualunque sua pari e concittadina sembrandole meglio provveduta e più sicura della sorte.

Stavano a questo punto le cose, e genitori e parenti s'eran condotti anch'essi, senza accorgersene, a stravolgere l'amoretto in impegno serio, quando Rinaldo cominciò a non farsi vedere o a comparire distratto, quasi addormentato. Non crediate che la fanciulla notasse il cambiamento: tutti in casa se n'erano accorti fuori di lei, che, tranquillissima, tutta presa dai suoi piatti lambicchi, trascurava da un po' di tempo, come una vecchia moglie, acconciatura, proprietà di vesti, e persino qualche abitudine di pretta pulizia personale, giungendo ad accogliere il giovane con patacche sul grembiule e unghie a lutto. Finalmente egli arriva un giorno con il piglio risoluto e un abito nuovo. « Parto » dice « lo zio vuol che finisca gli studi a Torino; per questo ero preoccupato ché non avevo il coraggio di dirtelo. Bisogna aver coraggio, tornerò per le vacanze. Intanto scriverò spesso, cara, e anche tu mi scriverai, non è vero? » Il discorso, proposto frettolosamente, e in tono sommesso, fra due porte, mentre i familiari fingono di non badare, ha un accento premuroso, ansioso, quasi servile. Ma se l'Ofelia resta colpita lo è, più che altro, per la selva di idee che germinano in quel punto dai rami delle sue ubbie segrete. Col capo accenna di sí, vagamente, la mano imprigionata da una stretta che vuol essere scongiuro contro ogni complicazione e protesta pericolosa. Le difficoltà che vede sorgere non sono l'assenza dell'amato, l'incertezza del futuro, l'ombra della gelosia, ma il senso coperto di questa ingerenza del canonico, gli effetti spiccioli del metter casa in una città sconosciuta e lasciar dunque i genitori liberi di svolgere ogni prodigalità in favore di Giorgio. « Non si avranno i polli e le uova dai contadini, pagheremo di più la serva »: questo arriva a pensare la scervellata e i suoi occhi perduti non si posano neppure un istante sul volto che reca in pelle una sentenza così chiara.

Le lettere da Torino furono, difatti, dapprima scarse, poi asciutte; alla fine diradarono ancora, cessarono affatto. La signora Ernesta, che fremeva d'indignazione, insistette per un congedo tagliente, drammatico. Ma la ragazza dura, e non per straordinaria tenacia di affetto, ma per l'attaccamento a quella specie di rimario della vita che aveva creato e battezzato coi suoi lumi: sorta di quadri di scrutinio per cui, sull'accessit consentito da quei tali sacri punti non c'era da contrastare. Una volta mantenuta nella propria latitudine, l'umiltà diventava cieca presunzione, più difficile a piegarsi di un'autentica superbia.

Naturalmente il congedo arrivò da Torino e fu espresso con ragioni e in termini non si sa se più goffi o crudeli. « Tu non mi sei mai piaciuta » concludeva testualmente il gaglioffo, dopo aver tergiversato fra la contrizione e una attitudine superumana che allora correva le strade. Fu questa frase che la colpì malamente. Il mondo vacillò: le quotazioni eran dunque false, l'esame non valeva, bisognava forse ridiscendere a una classe inferiore, fra termini di paragone ancor più modesti. Il dolore vero e proprio dell'abbandono, se ce ne fu, rimase soverchiato da questi pensieri: non un moto di reazione in quell'animo, ma un rinvilimento sonnacchioso che dava allo sguardo una svagatura più profonda.

A questa svolta, quasi avessero aspettato un segnale, le disgrazie cominciarono a piovere sulla ragazza. Malattia del padre, le prime scioperataggini del fratello, spese gravi e tristi che gettavano la madre nella costernazione. La vita in casa si restringeva intorno al letto dell'infermo, scartando a priori, come sacrilega, la rinnovata questione della fanciulla da marito. L'assistenza delle nottate e delle lunghe ore diurne lasciava scoperto e indifeso quel benedetto cervello talvolta assalito dall'angoscia, più spesso dal solito ticchio di smantellare l'avvenire. I pensieri non si contenevano, prendevano un'andatura sfrenata e cinica scorazzando in lungo e in largo, scavalcando la morte del malato, dandola freddamente per ovvia, trascorsa, dimenticata. Travolta dalla corrente l'Ofelia stentava non dico a lottare, ma persino a risentirsi, la velocità delle idee comunicandole una specie di capogiro. Quando però arrivava a controllarsi, a oggettivare l'eco di quel che le passava in mente provava moti di pentimento e di ribrezzo che le precipitavano nella disperazione: una disperazione cristallina, dentro cui seguivano a fluire, come sviluppi di cieche amebe, particolari di episodi nettissimi che continuavano per conto proprio la definizione del quadro da cui la volontà s'era distolta. Il padre morì, e la figliola si ritrovò ad aver calcolato esattamente quante bottiglie d'acqua gli potessero avanzare dall'ultima spedizione di Sangemini. Intanto piangeva come se non avesse previsto nulla, con una immediatezza da primo dolore infantile, schiacciata dal peso di una realtà che la purgava da tutti i mali umori e addormentava le smorfie del cervello stanco.

Più tardi, col vestito di lanetta nera, tinto in economia, e corto e stiracchiato ai polsi, si rimise a ragionare ad alta voce colla madre. Credeva di esser cambiata, di avere addosso tanta più saggezza e autorità, ma invece ripeteva senza avvedersene proprio le considerazioni di cui si pentiva due mesi prima: ricche di chiose pessimistiche e velate da un accento monotono che il lutto pareva comandare, ma in cui spuntava il tono dei vecchi soliloqui. Nella sparutezza della casa senza capo, si sentiva rinvigorita da un'acre soddisfazione, per il ritrovarsi davanti, indifesa ascoltatrice, quella signora Ernesta che aveva sempre vissuto sulla fama d'essere una perfetta donna di maneggio, e invece non era riuscita che a favorire gli sperperi del figlio: come ora i fatti dimonstravano. Ottenuti i conti delle rendite, conosciuta finalmente la situazione del patrimonio, la ragazza aveva sorriso per l'amara fierezza che i suoi calcoli si trovassero così ben confermati. Discorrendo del complicato testamento paterno e fatta ardita da quell'esserci scritta a chiare lettere, non si peritava d'incalzar la madre con domande indiscrete, crudeli. Come disporrebbe della sua dote? Quali le divisioni dei titoli in banca? La vecchia, offesa da quei segni di sfiducia e di poco amore, non mancava di ribattere con risposte piene di acidità, di rigidezza e di albagia: tanti colpi di frusta per l'ombrosità della figlia. « La villa va conservata al primogenito, all'erede del nome i mezzi più adatti a portarlo con decoro ». Furon tirati in ballo anche i diamanti della nonna: per Giorgio, anche quelli, quando prendesse moglie. Furiosa e lucida la ragazza ghignava: « ma come ho saputo indovinare! » Era ormai sicura di possedere un fiuto di volpe, e questa sicurezza precipitò il suo destino, ché nessuna titubanza si oppose al filo dei suoi ragionamenti.

D'un colpo l'avvenire fu sparecchiato di qualunque proposito matrimoniale. Lavorare, doveva, e nient'altro; o meglio sgobbare e penare come ai tempi della scuola per arrivare a qualche cosa. Giorno e notte pensava a come avrebbe potuto adoperarsi, evitando i consigli, non fidandosi che del proprio cervello. Intanto aveva impegnato colla madre una lotta a colpi di meschinità e di pitoccherie, secondandola, anzi precedendola sul sentiero dell'economia più taccagna. Licenziate le due domestiche, le due donne s'incontravano per le grandi stanze, piegate all faccende più umili e fastidiose; e si compensavano del proprio decadimento avvilendosi ciascuna in mansioni che dovevan suggerire all'altra mansioni più pesanti. Neppure una sciaquapiatti aveva tollerato l'Ofelia, e, aspettando di lavarsi da sé, poteva soddisfarsi alla vista della madre, nemica dei fornelli, impestata di fumo, in cucina. Messe su questa scesa non si sa dove le due donne sarebbero scivolate, se, alla fine, la giovane non si fosse pronunziata sulla via da seguire: caparbia, subito, e sorda a ogni rimostranza come se la decisione avesse un'origine divina.

A diciannove anni, con poche nozioni tecniche e nessun talento musicale, l'Ofelia cominiciò a prepararsi per il diploma di pianoforte. S'era prefissa il cimento più duro e più lungo obbendendo a quell'istinto della sua natura che le permetteva di rimanere esposta senza proteste alle angherie dell'avarizia materna; chiusa nel salotto dall'odor di canfora, senza fuoco l'inverno, soffocando d'estate: disarticolata nel busto e nelle braccia per le esigenze del metodo, su quel seggiolino tormentoso, i polpastrelli via via squadrati dai tasti. S'era procurata un piano tedesco di gran marca e andava una volta alla settimana a Firenze per ricevere da un maestro illustre delle dispendiosissime lezioni. In treno, per quella mezz'ora del tragitto, prendeva un'espressione così lunatica e assente che non le capitò mai di sentirsi rivolger la parola. Se la stanchezza e le preoccupazioni dello studio glielo permettevano, ingannava il tempo ripensando al costo dello strumento nuovo, a quello delle lezioni, dei libri, delle tasse d'esame: sangue suo, denaro tolto dalla sua parte dell'eredità paterna. In città non vedeva nulla, né gingilli, né eleganze, né fiori, correndo sulle scarpe mal risuolate, tinte al nero d'inferno, colla veste sempre un po' unticcia al collo e un po' infrittellata, ché in casa si misuravano il sapone e la benzina. « Disgraziata », la compativano le colleghe arricciando il naso all'odor d'agro che le trasudava di dosso senza abbondanza. La credevano poverissima. Essa poi di rado parlava con loro e le vedeva come in una nebbia, tutte seducenti e parate di quell'avventurosa forza cui la sua giovinezza non voleva pretendere.

Tornata a casa, si levava il vestituccio, le scarpe storte, riponeva tutto con cura, senza però toglier polvere né macchie; poi infilava la vestaglia sdruscita di peloncino, d'inverno il giacchetto a maglia, due ciabatte; e si chiudeva in salotto. Subito scrosciavano le misurate tempeste degli studi, interrotti venti volte, venti volte ripresi. Fra un'ora emergerebbe l'esile disegno dei rompicapo di digitazione, puerile tormento a cui la mano adulta si costringeva, impavida. Di lontano, nella fila di stanze disabitate, qualche tela di ragno tremava al frastuono, mentre, ridotta in camera, la madre tirava il filo e la saliva su un rammendo che non avrebbe retto a un solo bucato. Per lei imbruniva sempre troppo presto, anche di giugno, e allora, sospirando, si alzava e non trovava di meglio, per risparmiare il lume, che andare alla benedizione. A cena imbandiva alla figlia una larga e nera bistecca di cavallo « economica e corroborante » che quella mandava giù colla voracità di un serpente distratto. Era l'unica prova della premura materna che ritornava ogni sera, ugualmente inavvertita. Senza curarsi delle proteste dei vicini e delle buffe storielle che su di lei cominciavano a circolare in paese, la ragazza si rimetteva al piano anche dopo cena, al lume di una candeletta che le sciupava gli occhi, e pareva, sul coperchio del lussuoso strumento, l'omaggio di un povero alla tomba di un santo aristocratico. Suonava, in genere, dalle otto alle nove ore al giorno, e quando andava a letto piombava nel sonno a capofitto. Sognava raramente, e di musica mai. Qualche volta, specie nei primi tempi, si svegliava con la sensazione di un gran dolore alle mani e s'accorgeva di tenerle rattrappite nello sforzo di un passaggio difficile; senza che un suono, una voce sola sfiorassero il suo cervello.

Le stagioni passavano, e mai una volta le vecchie preoccupazioni di accasarsi riapparvero, anche di sfuggita. La testa di Ofelia non poteva contenere più di un progetto, né tornare indietro da sola e accoglier dubbi sul pensiero dominante. Il gusto della fatica, assaporato nell'infanzia, tornava a signoreggiare, e con esso una propensione allo scrupolo più meticoloso e intransigente. Il compito assunto prendeva le proporzioni di una sfida a una impresa colossale: ogni nuova settimana presentava la parete di una roccia liscia e diritta che sembrava impossibile ascendere e se la smunta duttilità delle mani finiva per trionfare, altre sfingi aspettavano affacciando questioni di armonia, di contrappunto, segni visibili di abissi minacciosi che avrebbero ingoiato la mente e l'orecchio. Pure la ragazza procedeva: distinguere in lei intelligenza da volontà appariva adesso impraticabile. Con questi mezzi i problemi più ostili consentirono a ridursi in una pillola assimilabile; le dita poi divenute martelletti precisissimi potevano obbedire a qualunque scrittura e graduare ogni effetto. Fu allora che il maestro cominciò a parlare d'interpretazione, in modo scoperto. Discorreva, come molti suoi pari, caotico e dottrinale, mettendo innanzi a ogni passo elementi di ambiguo senso, fra il tecnico e l'ultrasensibile, male intesi, peggio spiegati; ma tutti involti e protetti dal manto del segreto artistico. Allibita, Ofelia ascoltava e si credeva all'inizio di un nuovo tormento; ma la minaccia dileguò per incanto il giorno che, avendo assistito a una esecuzione celebre, essa seppe riprodurla al capello. Il maestro infatti battè gli occhi, immaginò di aver misconosciuto un talento e cominciò a tempestare che l'allieva doveva ascoltar musica quanta più potesse, per formarsi un gusto e uno stile. Docile, l'Ofelia buttò giù anche questo boccone delle spese per i concerti: non si divertiva né godeva in alcun modo, stando attenta come un cane e lavorando poi d'imitazione come un castoro. Per ora quelle parole di gusto e di stile non uscivano dalla protezione della tecnica e non la turbavano: soddisfatta di sentirsi essa a una continua prova generale dell'esame di interpretazione, e approvata. In realtà, dopo quattro anni di fatiche, non s'era ancor domandata se e come la musica le piacesse: quella lunga consuetudine di suoni pareva non averle proposta alcuna preferenza e appena aver inciso sulla sua corteccia sensitiva l'ossessione di qualche frase tematica, che, agguantandola in treno o per la strada, le faceva rimpiangere di non poter vuotarsi che attraverso un mezzo vocale impuro e quasi ridicolo.

Proprio in quel tempo arrivò, dopo anni di assenza, la cuginetta di Roma; figurava un tipo fuori via, così alta come s'era fatta e circolante con scioltezza angolosa nel panorama limitato dall'attesa degli esami ultimi. Era preceduta da una fama di intelligenza precoce che la malignità della parentela provinciale aveva allargato, insidiandola. Il liceo scavalcato di galoppo, fra poco l'università: un paragone sferzante. Aveva fatto il viaggio da sola, era arrivata all'improvviso, con certe valigie piatte dalla cerniera scattante completamente inedite per il paese, e pareva che scattasse anche lei ogni volta che muoveva il passo e la gonnella a piegoline intatte le si sciorinava nell'aria. Usciva ogni giorno prendendo un contegno da turista ironica, insisteva per trascinare l'Ofelia in campagna con merendine strafottenti, giusto per non perder l'occasione di canzonare la sua immane paura degli esami. In casa, apriva tutti gli usci, si sedeva sulle più foderate poltrone, né si peritava di frugare alla scoperta in un cassetto trascurato e di ridere sulle calíe che ci trovava dentro: il viso tagliente della zia Ernesta non le dava nessun pensiero.

Ma se l'Ofelia suonava, ch'era la regola, s'infilava in salotto senza rumore e le si metteva alle spalle, quieta, immobile, instancabile. Anche se non l'aveva sentita entrare, la suonatrice ne avvertiva la presenza per lo sfilacciarsi della propria attenzione e per una incomoda mobilità dell'animo. Tuttavia resisteva, si puniva con ripetizioni più del solito meticolose e pedanti; alla fine doveva pur girare il seggiolino, voltarsi. Il busto e le spalle ciondoloni sulla vita, le mani in grembo colle palme rivolte all'insù; ma gli occhi a poco a poco si levavano, perdevano la fissità, parevano pezzetti di spugna bionda avida di bere. E bevevano infatti. Quell'antico interesse per le qualità degli altri, ammirativo a controcuore, pieno di rammarico e di mortificazione preliminare, si faceva risentire. « Bravissima, magnifica », squittiva la studentella con l'accento della toscana spatriata che ai toscani veri par sempre di una ricercatezza insultante. E giù a forzar le leve dell'entusiasmo, un po' sinceramente, un po' per amor di forma spinta.

Ma chi le dava retta? C'era da investigare l'arco delle sopracciglia, quel neo sullo zigomo, il gesto del braccio, la cintura rossa, tutte cose scaturite dal fondo di un lusso scorrevole e senza peso, il suggello — pareva — di una classe disorientante. Nell'osservazione intensa, perduta, ribollente di pensieri e sensazioni indistinte, l'Ofelia affogava, appena in sensi per opporre alle lodi un goffo e stordito « ché ché », dove la volontà di asserragliarsi e difendersi entro i propri limiti si tradiva pietosamente. Il riapparire, del resto, di questi segni del suo vizio spirituale sgorgava appunto dalla difficoltà di catalogare un essere già creduto di un genere opaco e trascurabile e invece diventato tutt'altro, così vivace, prepotente. Nel disappunto della constatazione s'incaponiva a discerner come le linee di quel visetto si scomponessero da un momento all'altro e i contorni della persona non ricusassero nessuna prova. Mancavano i termi di paragone, non c'era neppur da capire se Giulia fosse bella o brutta. Poi c'era la questione morale, sociale: la cugina studiava, sia pure con insolente eleganza, ma per un fine pratico, per lavorare e guadagnare insomma; apparteneva dunque senza discussione alla classe inferiore a cui l'Ofelia stessa si era ridotta. Ma come riconoscerla eguale se nei suoi discorsi e nel suo contegno balenavano le pretese più insensate, e, in gran confusione, spiccavano orgoglio, intransigenze, arroganze, indulgenze e vanità, tutto annafiato di buffonerie e di risate insopportabili? « Via, non c'è sugo », fremeva tra sé, quando certi sfacciati attacchi alle celebrità più consacrate finivano coi pronostici della moda invernale; « non c'è da fidarsene ». A dire il vero aveva soltanto una gran paura di esser presa in giro. Le sembrava che i piedi, abbarbicati alla base dello sgabello, le crescessero mostruosamente dentro le ciabattacce. Sempre si era sentita modesta, non mai come adesso goffa e inerte, fuori di ogni ausilio, fosse per quello di una volontaria umiltà. Inoltre un prurito di battaglia, una rabbietta, vaporavano insolitamente a intorbidare il cervello e a suggerire che, dopo tutto, Giulia aveva poco da scherzare e valeva meno di lei non avendo nemmeno una dote, dei terreni, qualche soldo in banca. Spesso, accecata affatto, provava a vendicarsi e sceglieva il momento che la cugina, quasi giocando, metteva le mani sulla tastiera. La bocca piegata a un disgusto tutto professorale, coglieva e denunciava a gragnuola gli errori, i difetti, i viziacci di quelle dita estemporanee. Ma le frecce ricadevano senza forza, avendo ottenuto, se mai, d'allontanare il bersaglio che intendevano colpire. Meravigliata d'esser presa così sul serio, Giulia esclamava con enfasi: « lo so benissimo, sono un'assassina », e via a ridere dando vento al moto delle mani accennando temi e passaggi, canticchiando e dicendo intanto « che delizia, che splendore, devi suonarmi questo e quest'altro, quel largo in do maggiore è sublime »: voltata per metà, seduta di traverso. Poi di scatto, eccola in piedi: « Ofelia, piantala, si va in campagna a fare un bel giro che ho scoperto stamani? » E non trovare una frase per condannare quella superficialità, un motivo per ammirarla meno.

In serata, al lume della solita candela, quelle parolette, quei fervori smozzicati le ritornavano in mente disturbando la sua concentrazione o prendendo la figura di speciali segni d'intendimento. Certi motti con cui la cugina usava forzare la dignità di alcuni passi celebri e darla per banale e sorpassata non potevano cancellarlesi dalla memoria. Contrita, smarrita, sentiva di trovarsi nel nòcciolo di un mondo infido, sulla soglia di una porta di cui tutti potevano aver la chiave fuori di lei: per esempio quella ragazzetta che sapeva a piacere suscitare un sospetto di sgradevole dissentimento o insinuare l'allarme di un valore misconosciuto. Riusciva a calmarsi con difficoltà; e quando Giulia annunziò su due piedi la partenza, si sentí disintossicata.

Quella smania, quella scontentezza dovevano ritornare un paio d'anni dopo, quando il ricordo del diploma non era più che una pallida cicatrice e le esigenze del mestiere avevano consigliato una sistemazione nella città più vicina. La gioia del successo non aveva fatto che balenare, incalzata dal pungolo dei provvedimenti da prendere per la nuova vita. Risiedere in un centro importante era parso indispensabile, ma equilibrare le entrate alle spese era divenuto un assillo per la povera formica a cui mancava sempre il terreno sotto i piedi. La scontrosità aveva ceduto malamente alla paura di aver poco lavoro, e s'era vista un'Ofelia del tutto inerme, abbozzare un faccino cordiale per ingraziarsi quelle colleghe che, possedendo il segreto e la privativa delle lezioni ricche, potevano darsi il lusso di cederne qualcuna alle novizie.

Una fra queste, dall'aspetto accuratamente disadorno, di età matura e di una linda affabilità, le aveva ispirato gran fiducia, subito giustificata dall'introduzione in parecchie case che non lesinavano sull'onorario. Ma queste case si rivelarono strani luoghi, abitati da gente più strana ancora, tra cui la collega pareva trovarsi come il topo nel formaggio, prendendo un rilievo insospettato. La sua semplicità diveniva ermetica, quelle espressioni e quei modi dimessi che l'avevano attratta parevano riferisi a una specie di metafora onnipresente e celare un doppio fondo di sentenziosità sacerdotale. Non c'era voluto molto per scoprire sotto la calma e il quieto sorriso un clima di esaltazione e di cenacolo. Le famiglie che l'accoglievano e a cui Ofelia veniva man mano presentata sembravano anch'esse obbedire a leggi di disequilibrio metodico, giurato: e coi segni di una ilare e costante fratellanza respingere tutta l'umanità in un altro pianeta. Bambini dalle pelli angeliche, esponenti di incroci nordici più e più volte ripetuti si gloriavano con stridule voci di non aver studiato affatto, mostrando spesso disegni caotici o declamando canzonette un po' folli, rispettatissime dagli adulti; mamme infantili scotevano zazzere di sole e si rotolavano per terra coi bimbi e i cani, poi sparivano per mesi e si sapeva che erano andate a casa loro, in Norvegia, nel Canadà, in Australia; nonne in giacca maschile e colletto duro, fumavano la pipa, e domandavano ragguagli sui nipoti colla voce nera.

Tale fu e divenne sempre più esclusivamente la clientela di Ofelia: gente che portava nomi di una certa fama, di letterati, di artisti, e con essi un'autorità di sanzione intellettuale che la ragazza, colla sua innata reverenza per le posizioni fatte, non era capace di rivalutare. Per un poco stette in pena sul modo d'istruire degli allievi tanto diversi da quelli che s'era figurati, poi si abandonò ai vecchi metodi coscienziosi e alle proprie esperienze di scolara cocciuta, ed ebbe la sorpresa di sentirle portare al cielo come originali novità da quei pochi adulti che per capriccio ne prendevan cognizione. « Una signorina straordinaria », si cominciò ad annunciare in giro, colle varianti di « incredibile », « deliziosa », o « fantastica ». Tutti i coniugi italo-finlandesi o estoni o polacchi, di stanza in città, la vollero per i loro « babies »; e fu così che l'Ofelia rimase chiusa come un fringuello cieco in una gabbia troppo levigata piena di esseri disformi: e questa gabbia portava il nome che i borghesi hanno spesso in bocca e succhiano come una pasticca di lusso: il nome dell'arte.

Inavvertitamente questo breve vocabolo traditore comandò alla sua vita, dettando leggi oscure e perentorie: le parve di essere stata ascritta di sorpresa a una religione ignota e rigorosa. « Già, lei, un'artista... », diceva qualcuno un giorno; e la maestrina si sentì colpevole di truffa e chinò il capo avvampando di rossore. Quando ne ebbe il tempo fece uno dei suoi esami di coscienza, parziali e pedanti, e si ritrovò alla solita irritazione impotente contro il mondo che riusciva sempre a condurla dove lei non voleva. Si accorse che le davano noia tante cose e le individuò: quell'eterno uso di parole piane, semplici all'apparenza, ma calcate da un'insolente vibrazione che voleva imporre un sottinteso concordato in una cerchia di eletti, non mai spiegato però. Odiò a morte certi aggettivi indeterminati, tesi a ogni passo, nella lode e nella critica, a tentare l'onestà altrui; come « musicale », « ritmico », « istintivo », o soltanto « intelligente », « divertente ». Sembrava un gergo alla portata di tutti ed era invece uno scambio di lasciapassare, operato fra due scambietti rituali. Credere o non credere alla virtù di quelle magie? Malgrado la diffidenza, il rispetto per chi sapeva muoversi fra tanti pericoli con tanta disinvoltura, sgorgava così spontaneo che la diffidenza veniva travolta. Restava solo il dispiacere d'aver scoperto un'altra classe privilegiata e di non poterne far parte: perché lei, qualunque cosa apparisse dall'esterno o credessero gli astanti non consentirebbe a illudersi mai. Per disgrazia sentiva anche, in fondo a tutte quelle schermaglie non assimilabili, qualcosa di serio, di alto: un richiamo confuso che non le sarebbe mai giunto, ma per cui nessuno sforzo o fatica sarebbero stati perduti; il sospetto di un fluido e limpido potere di cui le smorfie dei suoi clienti non erano che un'ombra triste e lontana.

Il gioco incrudelì. Si sparse la voce che la « signorina straordinaria » non era soltanto una maestra originale, ma anche una esecutrice ottima. « Ma sul serio? » « Di tutto prim'ordine, ti assicuro, prova a farla suonare ». Di conseguenza l'Ofelia ricevette più volte inviti a passar la sera in quelle case, appena tollerabili nell'ora quieta delle lezioni e per le scale di servizio. Non osò rifiutare, e al chiarore di certe luci strambe si sedette dinanzi a pianoni illustri che lampeggiavano di boria riflettendo con malevolenza il suo viso spaurito: intorno immagini soffici di donne-bambine e di uomini sconsciuti e pulitissimi, ognuno devoto a formule di riservatezza e di espansione tutti particolari. C'era per aria, un'intesa di famiglia, un ostentato ricorrere di nomi di assenti, anzi di nomignoli dei più affettuosi, ch'eran poi quelli di personaggi importantissimi disseminati, per il momento, nei punti meno praticati del globo: Pucci, Bubi, Lulli, e altri simili. Non tutti la salutavano, anzi pochissimi, ma c'era sempre qualche donnina che per un minuto o due arrivava di fretta per coccolarla e strillettare volgendosi intorno: « sentirete se non è un amore »; e allora lo stesso sguardo tra benevolo e divertito stuzzicava tutte le pupille. Suonare con l'esattezza e la pulizia degli anni di studio, fu, per l'Ofelia l'unico riparo alla vergogna, alla umiliazione e anche alla paura di perder degli allievi. Sapeva che fra gli uditori c'erano spesso dei musicisti celebrati, ma non se ne sentiva commossa perché la sua convinta modestia la diffendeva. Badava a lavorare correttamente, come una buona operaia, sentendosi protetta dall'onestà del proprio lavoro. Ma quando scoppiavano gli applausi e doveva voltarsi, provava come un languore di stomaco, una specie di scuoramento. « È incredibile, è formidabile », ripetevano voci estranee al di là di quell'anello di vuoto intorno al piano e allo sgabello, che sarebbe pur necessario attraversare sotto gli occhi di tutti, prima di scomparire. Era sempre meglio rivolgersi di nuovo alla tastiera e suonare daccapo, anche se non richiesta.

Dopo, quando era riuscita a raggiungere una seggiola e smaltire alla peggio le più inevitabili congratulazioni, si vedeva dimenticata o trattata come un oggetto di curiosità o un bambino molto piccolo e probabilmente sordomuto. Anche si facevano, non molto discosto da lei, e a voce alta, discussioni e considerazioni paradossali sul modo di suonare questa o quella musica, e nessuno veniva a domandare il suo parere: anzi ella sentiva di tanto in tanto fare il suo nome e dire, per esempio: « è inutile, per Bach, per Mozart ci vogliono dei tipi così, senza temperamento, umili e cristallini ». Intanto, vedendosi osservato, qualcuno le lanciava da lontano un sorriso dolce come un confetto, e al suo orecchio non arrivava più che il solletico, di una conversazione inglese, quella stessa che fin dall'inizio della sera s'arrampicava con piedini di ragno per le pareti lisce, ed era servita di sfondo a ogni frase intelligibile. S'avvicinava il momento benedetto in cui la ragazza poteva, inosservata, alzarsi in piedi, retrocedere, scivolare fino al paltò, scappare.

Per le strade deserte, l'eco dei suoi tacchi frettolosi bastava a riempirle il cervello, ma l'animo sapeva che, dietro quel vuoto, c'era un disagio nero. Valeva la pena di aver faticato tutta la vita per conquistare una posizione netta, esatta, e d'aver preso ombra ai più tenui cenni di contrasto. Dov'era andata a finire la sua chiaroveggenza? Ahimé, appena la memoria ripresentava il cammino percorso, il paragone tra il suo stato d'animo dei primi anni di lavoro e quello d'oggi, impreciso e smanioso, la atterriva. Cosa pretendeva, insomma? Era un maestra accreditata, pagata bene, il suo sogno: e le salivano le lacrime agli occhi.

Un giorno capì: le circostanze e l'isolamento di studi troppo assidui l'avevan portata più su di dove non volesse arrivare, su una scala pericolante; e ce l'avevan lasciata, a mezza strada fra due punti fermi. Bisognava salire o discendere: ma discendere ora, oltreché amaro, impraticabile. Salire poi equivaleva a tuffarsi nel vuoto, oltrepassare i propri mezzi conosciuti, cioè prenderne una nuova conscienza e farsene strumento per la creazione di un giudizio personale che li avrebbe a sua volta valutati, forse condannati. Uscire dal miracolo tecnico innocente, dominare qualunque espressione, poter dire « mi piace », questo lusso: l'umilità ormai non sarebbe servita a conservar nulla. Così, seguendo a fatica il filo d'un'intuizione fievole fievole, a momenti Ofelia si riscoteva: chi glielo avesse detto di dover penare ancora e per ragioni tanto nascoste, confuse. Non più programmi stampati, prove definite e circoscritte, ma un impegno profondo e senza tempo, quello di cambiare sé stessa, di seminare e crescere germi misteriosi, aumentare a freddo la propria temperatura, infettarsi, quasi. Un simile proposito veniva tuttavia concepito senz'enfasi, anzi con faticosa rigidezza, secondo il vecchio còstume di questa natura abituata agli squilibri fra le astinenze di un regime di vita rarefatta e gli sviluppi di un'atletica volontà. Il cieco gigante che era in lei gonfiò i muscoli, e al povero cervello non rimase che obbedire. A tastoni essa ritrovò quei problemi interpretativi che ai giorni degli esami aveva sfiorato e schivato, e li affrontò di petto, così sprovvista di romanticherie e di retorica da pretendere una sensibilità di pura sorgente, pagando sempre con moneta fresca e cioè di persona e di intelletto. Confinato in un mondo di suoni, limitato e modellato da quelle onde, nutrito troppo riccamente dalle prontissime mani, il suo pensiero prendeva un'andatura assurda, da pipistrello che vola basso nel crepuscolo. I nervi si assottigliavano, ma si mostrarono presto affranti, sicché lo stretto nido cittadino del gran pianoforte tedesco conobbe tonfi di porte sbattute da una mano fredda e sudaticcia, e l'arcata rauca dei singhiozzi senza causa. La signora Ernesta che aveva seguito la figlia in città contando sempre i tocchi di legna e i pezzi di sapone, aprí bocca una sera per consigliare: « Perché non vai a Roma, dalla Giulia? Ci stai un mesetto, ti riposi e rimetti le spese del viaggio ». Per la prima volta la caparbia ragazza cedette a un suggerimento e consentì. Allo sportello dei biglietti sporse il denaro senza ricontarlo, allentata in una specie di sonno a occhi aperti.

Piacque alla Giulia, ventenne e ormai in posa di letterata, la novità della visita. Una nevrosi da eccesso di lavoro, sembra, a quell'età, un caso più interessante che triste. Essa andò alla stazione coll'ultimo cappellino e anche con quella vaga tendenza all'ironia che, vent'anni or sono, distingueva le studentesse di qualche pretesa. Si trovò davanti la solita faccetta molliccia, conservata dall'anemia, le solite cadene sbilanciate del portamento; e già si disponeva a maliziosi reperti sulla leggendaria taccagneria di famiglia, quando una stretta di mano intensa e l'inatteso gesto del braccio che cercava il suo braccio e ci s'attaccava, incrinarono la freddezza dell'osservatrice. Da quel momento Giulia si buttò all'affetto, sentendosi protettrice e infermiera, ma a modo suo, con un'urgenza febbrile e un pizzico di prepotenza. La sua voce non bastava a esprimere il calore delle intenzioni. Fin dal primo mattino Ofelia dovette seguire un regime di riposo forzato, di serenità a tutti i costi: buio fin alle dieci, piedi scalzi nel corridoio: ma una sera, le inclinazioni della piccola intellettuale presero il sopravvento e condussero l'ospite davanti al pianoforte.

Del resto nell'ambiente nuovo, sotto gli auspici di quel gratuito interessamento l'Ofelia suonava, per la prima volta in vita sua, volentieri; le sue dita miracolose si rincorrevano, giocavano coi ritmi diversi, godevano delle pause, scoprivano insomma una specie di ginnastica, di danza spiritosa e muta. A poco a poco i suoni si facevan sentire con discrezione e si esprimevano in armonia col linguaggio fluido di quelle movenze: nessuna ostilità era in loro, nessuna chiusura, ma un accento arrendevole, facilissimo, che commoveva dolcemente. Anche coi suoni si poteva dunque trattare da amici. « Che meraviglia », esclamava Giulia, e non sapeva dir altro perché quel modo di suonare liquido e di ombre così nobili non si prestava a un commento di frasi speciose, ma pareva un augusto sillabario, composto di lettere gemmate ed affabili. Veduto dall'alto, il viso della suonatrice, quelle povere gote gonfiette, quel nasino a palla, sembravano rinfrescati da una pace infantile, mentre la bocca semiaperta per il respiro frequente tradiva in modo più patetico le orme di un appassito martirio e quasi un broncio di pianto. Sentendosi guardata fissamente, Ofelia alzava gli occhi, le sue mani si fermavano: « Non ti pare che abbia progredito? », domandava con un cenno di sospetto e una inconsumabile umiltà, riattaccando subito, anzi ricominciando daccapo, come quando studiava. Preferiva cimentarsi coi romantici quasi per mettersi volontariamente in pericolo, giacché il dispetto di sapersi giudicata « senza temperamento » e dunque inadatta a quella musica, galleggiava ancora sul suo sconvolgimento. Ma anche qui ogni punta di malizia sembrava dispersa: non rimaneva che una molle licenza da eludere e da trascinarsi dietro, in trionfo.

L'eco delle ultime note durava a lungo nel silenzio, ma non somigliava allo squallido muggito che, a Firenze, accompagnava i suoi passi solitari fino alla spalliera del letto. Il brulicare dell'aria mossa dalle corde sonore pareva accendere nel suo spirito una vibrazione benefica, un piacevole eccitamento di ottimismo. Abbandonate le spalle alla poltrona, si sentiva nascere sulle labbra il bisogno di spiegar finalmente a qualcuno la propria situazione, il proprio stato di servizio, insomma: come credesse di aver fatto tutto quel che poteva e di aver allargato il cervello ricevuto dalla nascita, in modo che ogni cosa ci stesse con decoro. Qualche volta le parole le uscivan di bocca senza volere, un po' oscure, simboliche, cabalistiche: eran come il rigurgito dei suoi vecchi eroici errori, travasato, decantato. In Giulia poi queste espressioni trovavano un terreno di cultura ideale. Inclinatissima ai rompicapo della indagine psicologica, non le pareva vero di riscontrare complicazioni e misteri in una creatura considerata sino allora fin troppo semplice, sicché l'ammirazione per la musicista si univa al gusto del carattere interessante. Sostanzialmente inesperta, si adoperava a riscaldare, a covare quei germi apparenti di singolarità, dando loro un'importanza che faceva salire l'eccitazione di Ofelia. La conversazione fra le due zitelle procedeva a scatti e a silenzi, tutti modulati dalle pose interiori di Giulia: un capo d'opera di reciproca incomprensione che avrebbe forse spaventato un ascoltatore maturo e conscio del senso che potevan rivestire quei rotti sfoghi di Ofelia e la sua nuova euforia.

Coi giorni, quasi si fossero capite e accettate, le due cugine risolsero ed esternarono i loro stati d'animo, in atteggiamenti di tumultuosa attività. « Ma come ti giova l'aria di Roma », ripetavano i parenti all'ospite, sorpresa a parlare animata, a ridere per un nonnulla. Rideva infatti Ofelia, apertamente, e proprio con quel moto della testa all'indietro della cugina. Qualcuno notò persino che le due ragazze si somigliavano, e non c'era cosa più falsa che tuttavia, in quei giorni paresse più vera. La Giulia, con il suo cervellino avvampato, aveva deciso che ormai la cugina non aveva più bisogno di quiete, di solitudine, ma anzi di allegria, di movimento: che era poi il suo tenor di vita abituale. Collo stesso piglio di affettuosa prepotenza e sicurezza con cui aveva prescritto il riposo, manipolò ora ricette di attività agitata e continua. L'altra lasciava fare. Tutti gli spini della sua cocciutaggine antica e permalosa, eran caduti per dar luogo a una fiducia illimitata nelle soluzioni di colei che colla sola presenza l'assicurava del possesso di una persuasione indispensabile: quella di capir tutto, di aver domato finalmente il cilicio dell'inferiorità.

Studentesse e signorine di casa, tutte le amiche di Giulia, la videro per un mese e in ogni luogo con quella dimessa compagna al fianco. « Una grande concertista », ripetevano le intime, sempre pronte a coalizzarsi per una esaltazione che tornasse a spicco della compagnia: e la incantata Ofelia beveva a larghi sorsi l'interessamento di quelle giovani ignote, non vedendoci che un segno di giustizia, finalmente; conservando la vecchia ostinazione solo nel modo di accettare qualunque forma del mondo di Giulia. Nelle sale dei concerti romani, stordita dai riflessi d'un sole proprio d'oro, umettata dall'aria stopposa di un inverno troppo dolce, fra gli smanacciamenti rapiti di una folla femminile grassa e tepida, non cessava di sentirsi accompagnata, cullata, messa a letto. Se non riusciva a portare innanzi le sue analisi di ascoltatrice professionale non si sentiva diminuita, ma sollevata a un livello di superiorità che più e più forzava la mano. Per la prima volta in vita sua girava gli occhi sul pubblico, e scopriva le finte di chi, la mano alla fronte, figurava di concentrarsi e dormiva; le melensaggini delle infatuate ignoranti, le erudizioni delle fanatiche. La cugina era sempre alle vedette per scovare e segnalare alla beffa queste belle cose e per coordinare episodi da esser raccontati con sapore: pose anche queste, ma Ofelia non lo sapeva, come non indovinava che l'improvvisa serietà del gruppo e lo sfavillar degli occhi ai nomi di Stravinski e di Ravel, fossero altrettali ostentazioni. D'altronde non c'era modo e agio di riflettere perché i giorni e le ore non bastavano a quella specie di corso teorico pratico a cui Giulia pareva sottoporla di proposito: consigli, esempi, programmi senza posa formulati e modificati per lei. « Un'artista come te » diceva essa con un tono ovvio; ed Ofelia non ricordava neanche di aver tanto temuto e schivato un simile appellativo. Da questo inciso scaturivano infinite divagazioni, le più stravaganti, le meno adatte al carattere e alla situazione di lei. Anche queste erano ascoltate, anzi assorbite in modo globale, senza discussioni o messe a punto che avrebbero certo intaccato l'edifizio da Giulia construito con tanta passione. Lo avesse anche voluto, Ofelia non avrebbe potuto sostenere il peso della lucidità: la irruenza della cugina, infatti, quando si metteva a consigliar qualcuno, faceva un po' paura: insistente, ombrosa, pronta a convertirsi in risentimento se appena il protetto mostrasse di rifiutare una soluzione. Disarmata, senza più sospetti né ripicche corroboranti, essa lasciava andare il cervello alla deriva, contenta di appagar l'altra con segni tangibili di spregiudicatezza, come quello di tagliarsi i capelli a zazzera: un fatto per cui la fermezza del proprio coraggio le parve una gran cosa. Così otteneva di perder di vista una volontaria soggezione e dispersione, contrarie affatto al suo vero spirito.

Il giorno della partenza la raggiunse alle spalle. Sentiva che doveva voltarsi cioè ritornare in sé stessa e negli elementi essenziali della sua vita, ma non si risolvette a farlo. Da un'ora all'altra, in vista di quella immutabile del treno, rimandava questa specie di dovere, consigliata dall'istinto che insinuava che, per riconoscersi, il tempo non sarebbe mancato, ormai. Invece il rimorso di non saper tagliar corto e fare i conti prima d'affrontar la solitudine, le rese irreperibile qualunque gusto, recente o antico; e la voce stessa di Giulia, impegnata nelle ultime esortazioni, diventava rumore da captare e ricomporre. Come per un malefizio si trovò colle valigie intorno, a respirare il fumo della stazione e la polvere dello scompartimento. Aveva gli occhi inquieti e persi della sua prima giovinezza, tuttavia badava a consentire. Sí, avrebbe messo uno studio per conto suo, lasciando al fratello la cura della madre. Sí, avrebbe combinato un concerto nella tal sala, con quel tal programma. Avrebbe curata l'eleganza, si sarebbe data un po' d'aria, un po' di tono. « Ricordati », punteggiava la consigliera, guardandola di sotto in su coi suoi occhi allegri: ferma dinanzi allo sportello, ma ondeggiando per ozio dall'uno all'altro piede sicché al finestrino quel moto arrivava colla maligna monotonia del mal di mare. Parlava sentenzioso, condensato, baldanzosetto, fra il sottinteso e l'ironico, com'era costume del suo gruppo e come la presenza di estranei consigliava; senza accorgersi che il sorriso di risposta non era né schietto né semplice, ma patito e stirato dallo smarrimento. Dietro la schiena, infatti, Ofelia nascondeva le mani e se le asciugava col fazzoletto perché le palme le grondavano sudore come se stesse per sedersi al piano, davanti a una folla. Quando il frastuono e l'urgenza crebbero, la voce di Giulia si fece acuta e pretese di seguitare, tranquilla, il discorso dell'« aria » e del « tono ». « Capisci, bisogna avere uno stile; guai, noialtre donne, a lasciarsi andare alla banalità ». Il viaggiatori, oziosamente affacciati, cominciavano a porger l'orecchio e a divertirsi, ma la ragazza non pareva avvedersene, spinta su una rotaia d'infrenabile loquacità e quasi d'esibizione. A onor del vero essa non cedeva a istinti di civetteria volgare, ma a un curioso bisogno di sfidar le convenienze in progressione geometrica dell'oscuro timore di sembrare sfacciata. E poi era certa di fare opera santa e di avere forze ed esperienze enormi da prodigare. Rientrata in città, quando il treno fu partito, disse a un'amica: « sono sicura di mia cugina, è una ragazza in gamba, farà la sua strada ». Aiutatemi a esprimere com'era buffo e commovente, nel pronunciare quel virile « in gamba » il suo piglio di conquistatrice.

Ofelia intanto, sul suo sedile di seconda classe, fingeva di dormire, e col capo volto alla parete, piangeva. Senza saper perché, gli orecchi ancora suonanti delle incitazioni di Giulia, le era venuto in mente quell'inverno che il giovane Rinaldo le era accanto e un certo scialletto di lana celeste che portava allora e, coll'uso, proprio sul davanti perdeva i péneri. Ricordava d'aver pensato ogni giorno: « stasera lo accomodo », e di non averlo mai fatto; e piangeva.

Alla stazione d'arrivo, quella madre, veduta sempre a due passi di distanza colla statura dell'autorità, e, nei giorni d'assenza, favoleggiata insieme a Giulia come l'ostacolo per antonomasia, il nemico tradizionale, attendeva presso l'entrata, vicino al cancelletto di ferro e subito dietro il controllore: per non pagare i quattro soldi dell'ingresso, si sa. Com'era piccina, Dio mio, aveva un viso tirato e magro, color mastice, su cui la bocca non si distingueva. Allungava il collo tutto grinze che il trito giabò nero non arrivava a coprire, e non vide la figlia che quando l'ebbe sotto il naso. « O di dove sei passata? » domandò, e l'Ofelia ebbe l'impressione di non riconoscerne la voce, corrosa da una nuova instabilità. Le due donne s'abbracciarono meccanicamente, baciando l'aria invece delle gote. Nessuna delle due sapeva discorrere, raccontare, e se ne andarono a piedi, col facchino alle spalle, intrise di un disagio oppressivo e minaccioso. Poi la madre parlò, e fu quando dall'angolo della strada si distinsero quelle tre finestre, la centrale insolitamente illuminata. « Te lo volevo scrivere », la voce cercava la fermezza antica, « ma tutto ben considerato... ». Per darsi un contegno e giustificare la sospensione avvicinava al naso il borsellino mencio, mostrando di cercar la mercede per l'uomo. La figlia, senza fiato, taceva e aspettava. Infine, porta cautamente la moneta, la madre alzò gli occhi e quasi aspirando energia dalla vicinanza dei muri famigliari buttò indietro testa e spalle. Così portata, la maschera dell'autorità ricomparve sui suoi tratti e le concesse di articolare: « Insomma, Giorgio è qui con una ragazza e un bambino: da una settimana sono sposati e li ho dovuti mettere in casa ». A queste parole i lumi, nella stradetta squallida, si accesero di scatto e il passo del facchino che si allontanava parve esageratamente sonoro. Di questo l'Ofelia si ricorderà sempre.

È chiaro che Giulia dovette scrivere troppo presto. Seguitava i discorsi della stazione collo stesso umore e gli stessi lazzi. Esigeva notizie sulla « gran scena », sulle opposizioni del « cerbero »,[1] sulla scelta dello studio. Ofelia leggeva e si sentiva batter sulle tempie i colpi di seggiola con cui la cognata accompagnava il dondolío del grembo, culla provvisoria al bimbo che doveva addormentarsi. Si fregava gli occhi, sbadigliava: il sapore, l'accento di quelle frasi svaporavano, erano ormai irraggiungibili. Rimanevano i caratteri eleganti, la carta blù, un tono di forzata confidenza e richiami a cui l'orecchio restava insensibile. Le giornate di Roma eran così lontane da non affiorare che raramente e con lampi da cui il pensiero si distaccava subito. Gli ultimi tormenti, oppiati poi dall'esaltazione del recente ottimismo, parevano egualmente sepolti. Ciò che prendeva a vivere, a brulicare, erano invece le meticolose avventure della inaspettata convivenza, cellule moltiplicate sulla piaga dei rancori per il fratello scappato, per la madre inetta e ingiusta. E poi questa donna estranea, questa cognata! Antenne innumerevoli, vibravano, trasalivano ai continui sfioramenti, ai contatti necessari. Un'attenzione

[1] Nella mitologia greca un mostro canino con tre teste, custode dell'ingresso dell'Ade. Qui un riferimento alla madre d'Ofelia.

ostile, voracissima, succhiava i più piccoli gesti, i moti di quel viso, le linee delle guance, della fronte, della bocca. I denti apparivano troppo spesso, sfacciati. Una creatura simile osava ridere dopo aver saccheggiate le tre stanzette di Ofelia, pagate col suo lavoro. Parlava anche molto, aveva un accento di veneta leziosa che volentieri scendeva al canto appena la più piccola faccenduola lo autorizzasse. Quando s'incipriava si avventava a capofitto sullo specchio basso della toeletta, allungando e stirando le labbra per tendere la pelle. Quei suoi tacchi aguzzi non perdevano un colpo, e l'odore un po' acre dei suoi panni forzava i cassetti. Immagini che ricorrevano alla mente di Ofelia più che altro di sera, quando chiusa nella stanza del pianoforte, l'unica che avesse potuto salvare per sé, si stendeva sul sofà letto e rimaneva supina cogli occhi al soffitto e le mani intrecciate dietro la nuca. A quell'ora non poteva suonare, il bambino si sarebbe svegliato, e così la presenza del grande strumento chiuso e muto diventava difficile a sostenersi. In mancanza di meglio l'abitudine vecchia di rimuginare a lungo su fatti meschini, sproporzionati all'attività del cervello, si trovava fomentata, mentre un nuovo istinto nasceva che la portava a toccare le gotine e le ditoline increspate del bimbo se rimaneva sola con lui. Almeno poter cacciare tutti e tenersi il nipote per sé, giacché, c'era.

Giulia riscrisse, le sue domande infittivano, nell'ultima lettera compariva persino, dopo una pioggia di sollecitazioni, il sospetto d'un rilievo ironico. Allora Ofelia prese la penna. Intorno a lei urgevano i richiami della riaccesa vita famigliare, e mille contrasti ne sprigionavano che la solitudine studiosa aveva cancellati e ora tornavano a vivere coll'antico bagaglio e le nuove armi. Se il vecchio mondo risuscitava e prevaleva, come certi giudizi d'allora sarebbero rimasti nell'ombra? Così Giulia rientrò ben presto nei contorni della ragazza fuori classe, fortunata per prepotenza, pronta a pungere, a ridacchiare di tutto: quasi un'avventuriera. Fu facile convincersi che i bei consigli non erano che formule di pietà, di condiscendenza canzonatrice. La risposta fu dunque riservata, generica. Vi comparivano modi d'una correttezza provinciale, sostenuti e distanti, agli appelli si opponevano termini d'una modestia impennata, nella chiusa la riconoscenza diventava dovere, la simpatia consuetudine e obbligo di parentela.

A una tal lettera non ci fu replica e quando Ofelia, che non sapeva di aspettarla, si accorse che non sarebbe venuta più, il suo animo concepì il più cupo risentimento fra quanti ne avesse mai provati, quasi un astio. Fra tutti i suoi debitori, e Dio sa se credeva di averne, sembrò che Giulia fosse iscritta col maggior titolo: nel cielo della sua mente, ridivenuto basso e nuvoloso, passavano a volte, troppo illuminate e allegre, le fanciulle conosciute a Roma. Ridevano certo di lei, a quest'ora, animate e condotte dalla bacchetta di Giulia. Allora dal fondo della sua tristezza un gorgoglio di collera zampillava: come le avrebbe schiaffeggiate volentieri. E questa violenza era l'ultimo omaggio ai modi della parente rinnegata.

Per mesi stettero silenziose le due cugine, l'una difendendo dalle beghe di famiglia la brace del suo rancore, l'altra tutta fuoco e fiamme in un primo momento e poi tanto immemore e svagata da poter giocare senza simulazione colle equivalenze della generosità. In capo all'anno ognuna poteva credere d'esser ritornata al punto di prima, anzi di non essersi mai mossa, quando una mattina capitò a Giulia di ricevere una gran busta dalla soprascritta in bella calligrafia, che veniva da Firenze. Non era chiusa, come avviene per gli avvisi di pubblicità o le partecipazioni di nozze: e una partecipazione di nozze era, infatti, con su il nome dell'Ofelia e quello d'uno sconosciuto riuniti dallo stesso svolazzo. Gino Sarri, leggevano gli occhi di Giulia e il suo cuore si stringeva. Chi è costui, perché lo ha sposato, perché non me ne ha scritto prima? S'accorgeva a un tratto di non aver mai considerato con umanità la cugina, e, forse, nessuno. Un peso le calava sulle spalle, come una responsabilità diretta dell'atto definitivo consegnato a quel foglio di carta. Non un istante pensò a un motivo spontaneo, a uno sviluppo di sentimento. Il nome dell'uomo, corto corto, le suonava male: rivedeva la figura della sposa, quelle spallucce, quelle manine madide e lividette, come un po' torturate, e le collocava allato, chissà perché, un tipo d'omaccio spesso e brutale. Per essere rassicurata si precipitò a scrivere, chiedendo apertamente dettagli, esprimendo la premura affettuosa in termini che potevano benissimo leggersi per forme d'indagine indiscreta: aggiungendo dei tremuli auguri, e un regalone sontuoso: tutto quel che ci voleva per svegliare la diffidenza. Né fallì il segno.

Ofelia rispose a puntino, né presto né tardi, curvando visibilmente il capo sotto il giogo di ringraziamenti onerosi. « È troppo », diceva, « è troppo per me ». Poi diffondendosi senza abbandono ma con una serrata compunzione sulle qualità dello sposo: « posso chiamarmi fortunata — scriveva — d'essermi imbattuta in un ottimo giovane, commerciante specchiato, che insieme alle consolazioni del focolare mi offre garanzie materiali non indifferenti. E tu sai che in famiglia la mia dote non era sicura ». Dopo questa mezza confessione, aspra e involontaria, il discorso tornava a farsi guardingo e soprattutto insipido: appena se nel ricambiare gli auguri si poteva sospettare il proposito d'indirizzarli in un senso tradizionale: da sposa a ragazza che, a buon conto, non ha ancora trovato marito. Pensiamo se Giulia, con quel suo caratterino, fu lenta a reagire. Rise di sdegno, voleva risponder subito in modo altezzoso e sferzante e intanto strappava il foglio, sillabando freneticamente: « idiota ».

Poi all'improvviso si calmò, rivide un salotto di provincia e una tastiera coll'ottava centrale dagli avori consunti: e le venne da piangere. « Morta l'Ofelia, peggio che morta », esclamava asciugandosi gli occhi con quell'enfasi retorica che nelle forti emozioni trasuda dalle donne colte come l'inchiostro dai polpi. E non credeva di dir tanto giusto.

Quella grande indignazione le parve, qualche anno dopo, una deliziosa bambineria. Aveva preso marito anche lei ed apparteneva ogni giorno di più a quel genere di persone che, abbastanza acute per accorgersi di non avere addosso nulla di eccezionale, né intelligenza fuor del commune, né bellezza, né doti singolari, e sentendone d'altronde il rimpianto, si danno a rivangare il proprio passato, infanzia e prima giovinezza, intese a scoprirvi il segreto di quei presentimenti di genialità che non han mantenuto la parola. Per questi esseri certi paesi e oggetti, testimoni della prima età, divengon temi di inesauribili fantasticherie; essi non smettono di frastornare altrui col resoconto dettagliato di interiori primizie; e se per avventura si farà in presenza loro il nome del paese nativo, della villeggiatura, infantile, o si ricorderanno consuetudini dei loro giovani anni, li vedrete rapiti, commossi, estatici come davanti a un capolavoro, a una visione di paradiso. Tutto per compensarsi con retrospettive illusioni, della mediocrità attuale. Si sa come la gente abbia a noia un tal costume, che, per mancanza di uditori compiacenti, trova spesso uno sfogo in certi libretti di larvata autobiografia, specchio di nostalgie ben vive e di ambizioni non ben morte. Le donne, mature e oziose, eccellono nel prepararli.

Figuriamoci Giulia, avviata su questa strada, un giorno di casuale passaggio, dopo tanti anni, per il luogo d'origine della sua famiglia: il paese d'Ofelia insomma. « Dietro questa via c'è una piazzetta straordinaria, arriviamo fino a quella finestra »: il povero marito non poteva usar gli occhi e le gambe a suo talento, imbrigliato nelle staffe di quei lussureggianti ricordi. Le strade, rustiche e sonnacchiose, respingevano vigorosamente gli appelli, ma la allucinata, forzando gli aspetti dell'attualità, non cessava di peregrinare e commuoversi sulle orme perdute di una quindicenne dalla cintura rossa. All'improvviso, proprio sul momento di ripartire, con un « aspettami in piazza » eccola balzar dall'automobile e scomparire in un portoncino. In piazza, davanta alla bava di un aspro caffè, mezz'ora dovette sostare il sant'uomo. Esposto all'uggia dei visi curiosi e dei ghirigori istoriati dai monelli sulla polvere dei parafanghi, s'indignava, preparando accuratamente una bella intemerata. Venne la moglie, alla fine. Aveva un pallido broncio davvero puerile e bevve silenziosamente tutti i rimproveri. Risalì in macchina senza fiatare, ci rimase zitta zitta per tutto il viaggio, e pareva che il vento, o il mal di stomaco non la disturbassero più, come di consueto. Sulla soglia dell'albergo mostrò poi una premura, nelle minute faccende dell'attender ai bagagli, insolita alla sua pigrizia di donna un po' viziata. Il marito credette a uno dei suoi pentimenti eccessivi e cominciò a scherzare. Pentita era infatti Giulia, ma non di ciò ch'egli immaginava: un vecchio rimorso, vissuto appena qualche giorno, rifioriva su quel ceppo concimato dalle nostalgie. « Perché non le ho più scritto, perché non me ne son più curata? », si tormentava ancora a notte alta, rivoltandosi nel letto. E il giorno dopo, alle due di un pomeriggio piovoso era in piazza del Duomo ad aspettare il tram di Castello.

Là, in una specie di fattoria, stava l'Ofelia, a quanto le avevan detto: ridotta male, con due figlioli e un marito pestifero. « Pare che sia giù di testa » aveva rinforzato una vecchissima parente, tentennando il capo a bocca stretta; e quell'atto non poteva uscirle dagli occhi, ricomposto dagli scossoni del tram e dal dondolío delle maniglie d'appoggio pendenti al soffitto della corsía. Era veramente una trista giornata e Giulia ci trovava il suo tornaconto di espiazione: giuste le correnti d'ariaccia umida, buone le zaffate d'acqua sui vetri e quelle lunghe soste agli scambi che in altri momenti l'avrebbero esasperata. Fra uno scroscio e l'altro poteva distinguere le squallide casucce del sobborgo fiorentino, e, dietro una campagna bassa, sommersa dal fango: i pochi passeggeri, umile gente i cui panni sentivan di cane bagnato, tacevano o sbadigliavano o scambiavan sospiri. Sotto la pioggia anche le eterne ceneri dei ricordi e delle tenerezze commemorative s'eran freddate. Il bagnaticcio del pavimento, filtrando attraverso le suole, suggeriva la necessità, fra poco, di girare a piedi chissà quanto per strade e sentieri molli, sotto l'ombrello grondante e colle scarpe inzuppate; pure, su queste previsioni, la mente si gettava con un brivado di ribrezzo e di desiderio.

Fin qui la testa aveva, secondo in solito, fatto il gioco preponderante. Ma quando Giulia scese al capolinea e si ritrovò coi piedi nella mota, in mezzo a una strada deserta, mentre i poveri compagni di viaggio eran già scomparsi in varie direzioni, conobbe un tal sapore di ignorata solitudine che fu per domandare aiuto come se affogasse. Il tanfo del bar dove entrò per informarsi, l'abbandono dei tavolini e quel fiato tepido e gonfio di stagioni calde irrancidite la confortò e insieme la distrasse con richiami di una densità e di un clima quasi letterari. Ma come il povero nome fu sillabato dal cameriere e poi respinto dalla mossa negativa del suo labbro, lo smarrimento e l'angoscia tornarono. Era stato quello della « prima » signorina di S., avrebbe anche dovuto divenir celebre, il nome di una grande pianista, e ora, fra quattro case, nessuno la conosceva: forse non apparteneva più neanche all'elenco della borghesia locale. Questi riflessi possono far torcere un cuore, appunto, borghese; e il cuore di Giulia si torceva.

Le sue caviglie si bagnarono, poi le suole sottili e i piedi arcuati sugli alti tacchi; l'ombrellino, spolto di pioggia, rimaneva sempre fermo nel pugno guantato, come una insegna d'onore. Ora Giulia sdrucciolava per un sentiero che non finiva di scendere, con lugubre insistenza. Un carrettiere aveva detto: « Chi, la Sarri? Sta dalle mie parti, alla Casaccia. Prenda di qua e poi trova un viottolino e non può sbagliare ». Pare che la solitudine, in campagna, debba avera almeno il privilegio dell'aria fina e del bel panorama. E invece no, qui si doveva scendere a una bassura non sospettata, sicché le casarelle del paese credute dianzi in piano, alle falce di una collina nebbiosa, assumevano di lì aspetti desiderabili e sembravano disseminate sul monte con una ricercatezza signorile. Dieci minuti di fango viscido e il viottolo sboccò nella desolazione di una carrareccia di fondo valle, tutta sassi, fra la melma.

Davvero non si poteva sbagliare, la Casaccia era accovacciata nel punto più triste e basso: sembrava un grosso detrito torrentizio o un disperato tentavo di arginare e incivilire lo stradale. Spoglia d'ogni vezzo campestre, piuttosto che una cascina richiamava il disegno di un palazzotto paesano non finito, uno di quegli edifizi in cui si leggono gli sforzi di una ambizione mal posta e i colpi d'una sfortuna sguaiata. Per i troppi usci, tutti aperti, e alcuni senza battenti né intonaco, non si sapeva come entrare. Prima di scegliere, a un alzar d'occhio che fece, balenò a Giulia, sovrastante e vicinissimo, il ponte da cui il tram era passato prima di fermarsi: di lì grandioso, e, fra i veli di pioggia, fantastico come un gigante delle zampe di ferro. « Permesso, c'è nessuno? », ripeteva affacciandosi a quelle stanferne, e la sua voce malferma le pareva sinistra. Finché, azzardatasi in un cortiletto, avvistò sotto una tettoia di zinco una donna china a lavare e certo assordata dal rigurgito di un doccione che sgorgava sulla lamiera. A salti, evitando alla peggio le pozze e un nuovo scroscio, fu sotto il riparo e stava per chinarsi all'orrechio della lavandaia, quando questa si voltò ed ebbe un sobbalzo così violento che Giulia si trasse indietro anche lei, tutta rimescolata. « Chi è, che vuole? » domandarono una voce dura e due occhi selvatici, mobili come l'acqua. Ma Giulia dopo aver articolato: « la signora Sarri », non aveva più fiato. Le sue labbra sillabavano « Ofelia », ma non ne usciva suono.

Come fosse avvenuto il reciproco riconoscimento non afferrava neppure dopo pochi minuti, seduta su una poltrona a dondolo tormentosa, in una specie di tinello sgangherato. La suscettibilità della poltrona era pericolosa quanto l'immagine, dopo l'irrequietezza delle pupille, di quel gesto lentissimo della mano stillante sulla fronte, a cui era seguíto l'adunco strizzone di un abbraccio. No, non bisognava pensare a queste cose, ma comporre alla meglio il tessuto di una tranquilla conversazione fra signore di casa, la più modesta e banale, per carità, e appunto tanto rara, tanto preziosa. « Come va la mamma, dove sono i bambini? » Ma tutto vacillava, c'eran del vuoti spaventosi in quella faccia, e, nell'aria, dei vapori infetti da evitare: gli occhi, volta a volta spavaldi o maliziosamente aperti, eran come cani all'agguato di una povera lepre. L'inimicizia delle pareti, sporche e rozze, per i mobili chiari, di serie, da sposa cittadina, ancorché polverosi e sdotti; la traccia scomposta e frammentaria di quel ch'era stato ornamento o traccia di gentilezza domestica, domandavano l'attenzione e preparavano l'insidia. Colla lingua secca Giulia sentiva venir l'affanno: non trovava più parole e tutti i suoi sforzi si riducevano a un sorriso che le tirava le mascelle.

Per fortuna la porta si spalancò e due ragazzetti entrarono, fra i cinque e i sette anni, ma più grandi e robusti di quel che la loro età non comportasse. Apparivano riottosi, rustici, pieni di silenziosa indifferenza. Alla vista dell'ospite abbassaron gli occhi scontrosamente, e intanto andavano prendendo a calci, con gli stivalini fangosi, le zampe del tavolo. « Ma come sono belli », esclamava Giulia appoggiandosi tutta sulla loro presenza che dava l'illusione di un clima regolare. Sul volto della madre, contratto fino allora da un'altera attenzione, si aprì una schiarita che non scoperse che un fondo di grande sofferenza. Nella carezza sui capelli del più piccolo si rividero i polpastrelli quadrati, a martelletto, d'una mano che un giorno volava sui tasti, e anche gli occhi si riconoscevano ora, tondi tondi, colla pupilla appuntita da un generica interrogazione. Sulla testa del bambino Giulia azzardò una carezza alla madre e al figlio, e poi colse quella mano e la stringeva forte come se sperasse operare un miracolo. Senza parlare, Ofelia lagrimava, lentamente, sicché Giulia si mise a palpitare di speranza. Colla gola chiusa si provò a dire qualche parola calda, semplice, quanto più poteva tranquilla: le lagrime continuavano e la fisionomia sembrava più tenera, più abbandonata. Allora, sotto il pungolo di quella speranza, Giulia, senza avvedersene, cominciò a discorrer fitto e troppo animato. Ricordava i vecchi tempi, il viaggio a Roma, faceva affettuose proposte: « vieni tu coi bambini » diceva, « sei un po' sciupatina, ti rimetterai in salute » e il suo parlare divenne così pressante che davvero un'eco dei lontani giorni tremò nell'aria. Se ne pentì quando vide che Ofelia, asciugatasi gli occhi, si metteva ad ascoltare con lo sguardo mobilissimo del primo approccio; e più quando il consenso si dimostrò con una voce eccitata e misteriosa. « Ora non c'è e non ritornerà fino a stasera » confidava quella voce. « Spie non ne ha lasciate, se n'è dimenticato. Bisogna impedirgli il resto, ricuperare i soldi della dote e portar via il contratto di vendita. Se mi aiuti a scappare mi metto in mano di un avvocato... ». Era Giulia adesso a piangere.

Non ne poteva più, e voltava la testa in modo che i bambini non potessero vederla; ma quelli in un angolo, s'eran messi intorno a un gatterello magro e vociferavano. A un tratto uscirono correndo, dietro la bestiola.

Nel silenzio, la foga concitata dell'inferma decrebbe, parve calmarsi: le parole stillarono lente, stagnarono affatto. Aveva cessato di piovere e dai vetri senza tende un laghetto di timido celeste rasserenava il tramonto. Con un atto immemore, ma disinvolto e arioso come non ne aveva mai praticati da sana, Ofelia si alzò andò alla finestra, ci appoggiò la fronte e stette immobile, simile a un donna che gode un po' di luce e di riposo dopo essersi accanita tutto il giorno al lavoro. Pareva che si credesse sola, e invece di lì a un momento la sua voce si levò, diversissima da quella di poc'anzi e nemmeno eguale a quella della giovane Ofelia. « Però come mi trovi ridotta », scandiva sopra una tessitura di commiserazione placida e quasi di riso, mentre la testa, contro i vetri non si muoveva. « Figurati che mi colgo a credere al malocchio, alle fatture, ai sortilegi. Come s'arrabbierebbe il babbo se mi vedesse. Fu l'allattamento del piccolo, capisci; da allora non son stata più bene, e del resto ho sempre avuto la testa un po' stretta. Ti ricordi di Roma, dei concerti, del mio lavoro? È stato il meglio della mia vita, ero così intelligente, capivo tutto ». Le ultime parole furono dette coll'accento spoglio e distaccato d'uno che legge, commemorando un morto di tanti anni.

La luce, calando, pareva accompagnare l'eco di quella umana saggezza per farla durare quanto più fosse possibile. Dietro al gatto anche i bambini ritornavano, e il più grande, biondo e atletico, d'un tipo che a Giulia non rammentava nessuno di famiglia, le si fermò accanto, e dandole di gomito, accennò col mento alle spalle della madre, mentre la bocca si torceva in un ghigno buffonesco e la manina, oscillando dinanzi alla fronte, spiegava il moto dileggiatore degli occhi celesti. Ma a piangere, ormai, non c'era più senso.

Stettero ancora un poco le due cugine, l'una sempre voltata, ritta e assorta, l'altra seduta e affranta: quasi occupate a respirare in pace la stessa aria per l'ultima volta. Poi, con prudenza infinita, Giulia si alzò, raccolse le forze per annunziare: « Devo andarmene, il tram parte a momenti, tornerò presto »; ma come obbendendo a una ingiunzione tacita non s'avvicinò alla finestra. Allora, vicino a quella testa opaca, comparve, pendula e colle dita arricciate all'infuori nel segno dell'addio, una mano cinerea. Ripeteva il gesto a intervalli equali, con un abbandono che imprimeva alle falangi una oscillazione ritmica: sembrava che palpasse alla ceca le corde d'uno strumento invisibile.

LE DONNE MUOIONO

Il 16 luglio 2617, a Valloria, città lacustre presso le rovine dell'antica Venezia, tale Mariano Pietrangeli, fu ricoverato in una clinica sperimentale per malati de mente. Era un ragazzo di vent'anni, di professione studente, e la sua anormalità fu definita di visionario lucido, anzi logico. Ragionava benissimo e, fino ad un certo punto, deplorava coi medici quella che non rifuggiva dal chiamare la sua infermità. Tuttavia, proprio nei momenti che meglio si adoperava per analizzarla e dominarla, lo vedevi battersi la fronte come uno che all'improvviso viene assalito da un ricordo preciso ed urgente, e giù a ragionare di cose e di fatti di cui nessuno dei presenti aveva nozione. Anche il suo linguaggio si alterava, egli si esprimeva con termini antiquati, quasi leggesse da un vecchio libro: ed era da notarsi come soccorresse allo stupire degli astanti traducendo in lingua corrente le espressioni meno comprensibili che gli uscivano di bocca. L'accesso non comportava furori, ma una specie di fervore appassionato che investiva particolarmente nomi di persone e di luoghi, rilevati dagli attributi di « papà », « mamma », « figlio mio », « la mia casa »: e simili. Qualche lacrima spuntava sul ciglio del giovane quando tentava di spiegare il suo dolore, convinto che quelle persone, quei luoghi tanto cari, non li avrebbe ritrovati mai più. Dopo, rimaneva, non depresso e attonito, piuttosto pensieroso e melanconico, memore di tutto quel che aveva detto, ma, in un certo senso, rassegnato alla necessità di non tenerne conto. « Eppure son cose vere » ripeteva di tanto in tanto, scrollando il capo come un vecchio. Sospirando, ma cercava di riprendere interesse alle cose dell'età sua, facendo progetti e ritornando quasi allegro. Docilissimamente si prestava agli esami dei medici, ma, col tempo, e valendosi della constatazione che il suo stato non mutava, cominciò a chieder loro di esser lasciato libero di convalidare o meno, con un esperimento pratico, la consistenza delle sue visioni. « Vi assicuro, sento di poter dirigermi senza guida: se non ritrovo quella casa cogli olmi, quel profilo di monte e la fontanina a mezza costa, verrà dire che son pazzo davvero e farete di me quel che credete ». Naturalmente i medici dissero che l'ammalato peggiorava, anche perché in tali proposte egli metteva una insistenza lagnosa, simile a quella con cui i bambini pregano di essere accontentati in un capriccio; e che i sanitari giudicavano segno di uno stato ormai cronico. Per placarlo, gli si concesse maggior libertà nel giardino della clinica e gli si lasciò anche scrivere, all'indirizzo di lontani paesi, lettere che chiedevano alle amministrazioni locali notizie di antichissime famiglie. S'intende che queste lettere non venivano spedite.

Non finiva l'anno e dodici altri casi di analoghi vaneggiamenti, tutti in soggetti di età giovanile, si manifestarono nella stessa città, che non era molto popolata. I ragazzi visionari credevano di ricordare, anzi « ricordavano » schiettamente quello di cui sino al giorno innanzi non avevano avuto cognizione o notizia: ognuno casi luoghi e persone diverse, quasi fosse profugo da un paese differente e sconosciuto. Alcuni, asserivano di chiamarsi (precisavano: di essersi chiamati, prima d'ora) così e così: nomi, la più parte, stranieri e in disuso. Furono messi sotto osservazione rigorosa e si notò che, a differenza del Pietrangeli, conservavano in quel loro divagare una baldanza e quasi una strafottenza più che giovanili. Per tutto il mondo ormai la vicenda, che cominciava a chiamarsi epidemia, era seguita con interesse nervoso e allarmato. Corrispondenze da Valloria si diffondevano a lungo sui primi sintomi e sullo svolgimento della nuova malattia e raccontavano per minimi particolari come, per esempio, nel corso di una conversazione elementare, quei ragazzi rompessero all'improvviso in suoni del tutto oscuri, ma senza mutare il tono del discorso, talché si capiva come l'avessero continuato in un idioma noto a loro soltanto. Il peggio fu quando, sui primi del '18, i dodici casi diventarono trenta, cinquanta (se pure ci si poteva fidare delle statistiche) e l'allarme minacciò di traboccare in pànico. Così sarebbe avvenuto sicuramente se qualcuno, che non era medico, non avesse fatto osservare come, dopo tutto, quella sorta di pestilenza non potesse far paura, dato che i giovani ammalati rimanevano perfettamente integri, capaci di lavorare e divertirsi senza sforzo né pregiudizio della salute. « Non sarà un centinaio di stravaganti a cambiare il mondo ». Bastò questa nota di semplice buon senso perché l'opinione pubblica passasse dal pessimismo più nero a una specie di euforia, tanto che prevalse il consiglio di non internare i malati (s'era parlato persino di lazzaretto) ma di tenerli d'occhio e di assisterli, quando ce ne fosse bisogno, nelle case loro. Anche il Pietrangeli fu restituito alla famiglia.

Questione di giorni, e i casi dilagando ormai senza controllo, divenne convinzione popolare, debolmente combattuta dalla Facoltà, che di malati non si fosse mai trattato, bensì di una meravigliosa conquista cui l'umanità fosse giunta per merito dei grandi progressi compiuti negli ultimi cento anni in fatto di igiene e di educazione razionale. Si appurò che i giovani visionari erano i primi soggetti su cui s'era sperimentato, nell'infanzia, un famoso e ormai comunissimo siero preventivo delle malattie nervose, le uniche fino allora resistenti ad ogni scoperta della scienza. Ecco il resultato del siero, diceva ancora qualche pessimista, profeta del malaugurio, i nostri figli diverranno tutti pazzi per suo merito; ma non c'era chi non gli desse sulla voce, interpretando le visioni dei giovani come un passo innanzi nell'approfondimento della coscienza individuale e collettiva su cui gli studi si sarebbero di certo pronunciati favorevolmente. Accadde intanto che un falegname, vedovo e padre di un unico figlio colpito dalla nuova malattia, invece che in analisi cliniche e in consulti inutili, decidesse di spendere il suo denaro in un viaggetto di qualche centinaio di chilometri, verso una località che il ragazzo non si stancava di nominare, chiamandola paese nativo e centro dei suoi affetti. Partì, dunque, col figlio, lietamente, come si recasse in vacanza. Al suo ritorno si presentò a un giornale cittadino per dichiarare che i fatti e le circostanze di luogo citati dal figliolo erano esattissimi. Esisteva ancora, intatta e riconoscibile, la casa che egli descriveva come propria, né era mutata la configurazione della via dove essa sorgeva: una strada antichissima, monumento illustre e prezioso. Negli archivi del Comune, rimasti miracolosamente indenni, malgrado le distruzioni di tante guerre, era ancor registrata l'esistenza anagrafica della famiglia che l'aveva posseduta seicent'anni innanzi, e il suo cognome era quello che il giovane aveva rammentato. Persino della morte di una bambina cinquenne che egli ricordava come sua figlia, amaramente pianta, perita in un bombardamento (colla testina schiacciata, diceva lui) fu rinvenuta traccia, e nell'anno preciso da lui segnalato: il '43, diceva: e si trovò scritto: 1943.

A questa notizia, diffusa immediatamente in tutto il mondo, mentre i medici scuotevano la testa e si scandalizzavano, ma a bassa voce, che ancor oggi dovessero deplorarsi fenomeni di leggerezza e di suggestione collettiva così rudimentali, si verificò un numero stragrande di partenze per ogni direzione: per settimane uffici ed opifici non furono in grado di funzionare e il traffico aereo fu decuplicato. Malati e parenti di malati si sparsero per ogni dove alla ricerca di una conferma simile a quella che aveva premiato il candore del falegname. Fu assodato in quella circostanza che il cosiddetto morbo era assai più diffuso di quel che non si credesse e che, insomma, tutti i giovani sui vent'anni ne erano più o meno tocchi. Nei mesi che seguirono il resultato di quei viaggi fu reso pubblico in una serie pressoché infinita di resoconti che ogni foglio stampava, ogni radio trasmetteva e ognuno leggeva e ascoltava, commentandoli, ponendoli in dubbio, diffondendoli. Molte favole inventate di sana pianta abbellivano quelle narrazioni, ma bisogna dire che, nella maggioranza dei casi, documenti ineccepibili stavano a provare la verità delle vicende e l'esattezza di quella che si definì « la seconda memoria ». Non mancavano, a commuovere gli animi già tanto eccitati, le voci di coloro che, nel rammemorare, si accorgevano di riferirsi ad epoche troppo remote, a luoghi radicalmente distrutti e mutati: gente per cui i viaggi non porterebbero ad alcuna conferma e certezza. Essi se ne rimasero fermi e un poco tristi, ma, nel silenzio della città spopolata, tanto più padroni di una sicurezza che garantiva il definitivo riscatto della sorte umana. Non poche furono le scoperte favorite dal nuovo patto fra l'uomo e il tempo: i giovani non si riferivano soltanto a nomi oscuri, a località perdute, ma anche a casati illustri, a luoghi e personaggi celebri la cui memoria veniva lumeggiata in modo del tutto inatteso, guida agli storici nelle loro ricerche. Venne il momento che nessuno, neppure i medici e gli scienziati più scettici, dubitò più rimanendo ovvio che per una via non ancora rintracciabile i giovani prendevano coscienza di una lora vita anteriore alla presente, e, talvolta, di più vite. Un clima di esaltazione fra mistica e paganeggiante accese la città: quell'unica sinora visitata da tali fenomeni. Forestieri di ogni paese vi accorrevano, spinti dalla curiosità, ma più dall'ardore di studiare il modo per cui anch'essi potessero riconscersi partecipi di un privilegio che non si vedeva perché dovesse toccare a una minima parte del genere umano. Furono compensati, il fenomeno della seconda memoria si allargava ad altre città, a intere regioni e fu un tripudio inaudito quando dall'America e dall'Australia giunsero le notizie dei primi casi. E cominciarono ad arrivare gli escursionisti sentimentali, quelli che venivano a ricambiar la visita di chi s'era scoperto un loro remoto affine, dagli occhi adolescenti, ma dall'animo percosso di echi secolari. Tardissimi pronipoti settantenni s'imbarcavano per stringer legami più profondi con un proprio trisavolo di ventidue anni: che li assicurava, oltre tutto, di una immortalità che la loro memoria, purtroppo, non era più in tempo a registrare, Discendenti di spose morte sul fior degli anni non trovavan pace finché non si avvicinassero a chi racchiudeva l'animo di uno sposo invecchiato in lacrime e morto fedele. Ne sorsero, nei primi tempi, complicazioni e confusioni sentimentali che minacciarono e spesso distrussero la coesione degli affetti presenti, avvelenati da nostalgie di ogni maniera e da una specie di oscillazione dei sessi. Qui sta il punto. A due anni di distanza, infatti, dall'inizio di questi avvenimenti, non ci si poteva illudere sul peso di una constatazione unamine e universale: nelle donne, nelle ragazze, la grazia della seconda memoria non s'era ancor prodotta, esse non riuscivano ancora a ricordare: pareva non ne avessero la forza e, forse (si cominciava a insinuare), la ragione.

Il fatto venne dapprima commentato leggermente, come una curiosità, giacché non si dubitava punto che, presto o tardi, anche le donne si risveglierebbero: ci si scherzava, anzi, con quel gioco di motti facili, sul limite della paterna benevolenza, che tutte le età hanno usato a proposito del carettere femminile. Il presentarsi ormai regolarissimo del fenomeno nei soggetti maschili rendeva d'altronde, a dispetto di quel che potrebbe sembrare, trascurabile un'eccezione pur tanto cospicua: talché le numerosissime donne che se ne occupavano pubblicamente, facendo ipotesi sulle cause di un ritardo così inesplicabile, principiarono ad esser sopportate male e quasi compatite. Vedetele, diceva più d'uno, il mondo s'è liberato dal suo incubo millenario, il fantasma della morte è sgominato: e loro, egoiste e piccose, non dànno tempo alla natura di operare! Forse per il timore d'incorrere in tali critiche, ma più verosimilmente consigliate da un arcano senso di pudore doloroso, le donne mostrarono di trascurare, tutto a un tratto, quel problema essenziale. Soltanto fra amiche sicure o tra le pareti di circoli strettamente femminili era ammesso che se ne parlasse, ma anche allora, cautamente, sospettosamente. Qualcuna sospirava, altre buttavan là una parola di amaro pessimismo, rievocando il nero destino della donna nei passati secoli: che, creduto ormai superato, ritornava oggi sotto il segno di una esclusione fondamentale. Molte protestavano, quasi superstiziose, contro questa forma di rinuncia aprioristica e ripetevano a sazietà, fanatiche, gli argomenti della speranza, della certezza: fra loro si distinguevano, per fede accanita, le madri di ragazze. Non era raro, infatti, che una fanciulla di umor vivace e gioioso, cambiasse carattere il giorno che il fratello principiava a mostrare i primi sintomi della seconda memoria. La vedevi raccogliersi per covare lunghe ore del giorno il viso del giovane, le sue labbra che quasi meccanicamente profetavano all'indietro, quella fronte liscia e consapevole del miracolo. Fra i membri della famiglia, era lei la più attenta e sagace a districare il senso delle sue reminiscenze dapprima oscure e che man mano si andavano chiarendo: spesso aiutata dalla sorellina minore, già ansiosa, sebbene inconscia. Quando poi la crisi entrava nella solita lucidezza felice, l'assistenza fraterna si risolveva in un cupo e quasi arcigno appartarsi. Chiusa in camera come le ragazze d'altri tempi, la giovane divorava in soltudine il suo silenzio interiore, quello sgomento di sentirsi chiusa nella breve vita d'oggi, una vita che le sembrava disprezzabile e da gettarsi, dacché era la prima e l'ultima che le sarebbe toccata. Antichi e scavalcati rancori della condizione femminile risorgevano per questa ingiustizia della natura, questa sordità del destino. Fra poco tutti gli uomini della terra avrebbero goduto la certezza di rivivere, di perfezionare le loro predilezioni, le loro doti, in un futuro senza posa rinnovato, mentre le donne si sarebbero trovate oscure ed effimere come farfalle notturne, incapaci di oltrepassare un termine che, al confronto, sembrava imminente come l'alba del condannato a morte. A questa realtà, che nessun fatto contraddiceva, non restava altro rimedio che uno stoicismo spinoso, tanto più difficile a sostenersi quanto più il mondo sembrava avviarsi a rinnegarlo, insieme ai dettati delle più austere filosofie. Era una pena constatare come frequenti fossero ormai le rotture di promesse, gli amori brutalmente disdetti. Qualche volta erano i fidanzati a provocare questi accidenti, per quel nuovo dividersi fra l'antica condizione e l'attuale: oggi fedelissimi e devoti, domani assenti, lontani, tutti presi da immagini e nostalgie irrequiete, irretiti nei modi dell'animo antico e che si rinnovava, straniando l'uomo attuale da quelli che erano stati i suoi gusti e il suo carattere e lanciandolo, per così dire, nelle irrimediabili dissipazioni dell'eternità. Ma sempre più spesso furono le giovani a spezzare legami che non potevano più reggere fra esseri di così diverso destino. Le loro decisioni erano irrevocabili, esse si rifiutavano a spiegazioni che, dicevano, erano inutili, dato che l'amante non sapeva o non voleva indovinarle. Né avevano torto, le poverette, sebbene qualche volta l'insistenza dell'uomo non fosse cecità egoista, ma gentilezza pietosa e magari intenzione di risollevare una speranza perduta. Le più ardite dicevano chiaro e tondo, con una voce gelida, di non sentirsi disposte a un episodio che per l'uomo sarebbe trascurabile; e le più innamorate, piangendo, ma pur riuscivano a staccarsi dall'amato e pregavano: ricordami, almeno, quando rinascerai.

Gli anni passarono a decine senza che l'esclusione per le donne dalla seconda memoria fosse contestata da un solo esempio; e sebbene gli ottimisti andassero ripetendo che il non rammentare una vita anteriore non toglieva la possibilità di rinascere o esser già nati, i costumi seguitavano ad alterarsi, come se la certezza fosse proprio all'opposto. Quella che i faciloni avevan giudicata, in un primo tempo, dispettosa suscettibilità femminile e impazienza irragionevole, si consolidò in attitudini di timor selvatico o di spavalderia ostentata: due aspetti che tradivano le inclinazioni antitetiche a cui il genere femminile s'incamminava. Nei laboratori, nelle cliniche, per l'innanzi servite alla pari da scienziati e scienziate, da medici e medichesse, si andò verificando gradatamente ma inesorabilmente, una discriminazione fra i sessi che la diversità dei fini divideva. Così, mentre gli scienziati si applicavano a cercar le riprove e gli sviluppi di quella che era ormai considerata evoluzione naturale della specie umana, le scienziate lavoravano febbrilmente e in segreto a scoprire l'ostacolo che le privava del grande acquisto: esse giuravano di riuscire e le capitane dell'industria, ancor numerosissime in quegli anni di trapasso, sottoscrivevano somme ingenti per finanziare i loro studi. Ragazze di ogni specie e inclinazione si offrivano in folla ai più rischiosi esperimenti e spesso perdevano la salute, senza poter gettare lo sguardo avido che sul loro misero passato di bambine.

Verso il '70, scarse erano le donne che accettavano di accasarsi. Prosperavano invece, sempre più numerosi e accreditati, certi istituti fra il collegio e il club dove esse, sotto vari pretesti, si rifugiavano: ed avevano il carattere di associazioni basate su norme speciali di vita e di contegno, sorta di chiese senza confessione, almeno esteriormente. Correva infatti voce che dottrine particolari li reggessero e vi si coltivasse una fede. Il mito arcaico di Eva colpevole e punita vi serpeggiava, a insinuare che certo la donna aveva peccato più dell'uomo, con maggior coscienza, e bisognava dunque che più dell'uomo soffrisse per meritare l'eternità del ricordo. In determinati periodi dell'anno le adepte si dedicavano a pratiche di raccoglimento interiore, di contrizione, seguite da una ginnastica della memoria portata sino all'esasperazione mentale. « Ricordate, sorelle, ricordate » suonava a misurati intervalli nelle nitide sale di quei ritiri, più simili a palestre che non a cenobi, una voce dolce e malinconica. Le ragazze chinavano il viso fra le palme, si premevano gli occhi lasciandosi penetrare dall'eco lunga di quella esortazione fanatica ed estenuante. Fra quelle mura portavano tutte sul capo un velo nero, come le antiche monache: e molte eran quelle che dopo averle frequentate con assiduità, lasciavano definitivamente la casa paterna, prendendo alloggio in stanze di cui l'associazione disponeva, simili a celle.

Di tanto in tanto si spandeva la notizia che un caso di seconda memoria fosse apparso in uno di quei singolari collegi ed era vero infatti, che, all'improvviso, una qualche fanciulla anemica, indebolita dalla pratica di un costante sforzo nervoso, usciva a dichiarare di avere ottenuto la luce, di « ricordare ». Erano racconti allucinati e finivano in parossismi: vi si notava un carattere di immaginazione del tutto affine a quello della sognatrice, e una sovrabbondanza di avventure, nella supposta vita anteriore, che bastava a destare il sospetto d'innocente mistificazione. Di regola, queste crisi si concludevano in singhiozzi disperati, in gemiti di confessione: no, non è vero, non ricordo più nulla, mi sono sbagliata, ho mentito! La ragazza era messa a letto, sopita con forti calmanti, e l'indomani, restituita alla famiglia. Ma quale famiglia. Madri taciturne o svaporate, padri e fratelli insensibili, tutti presi dal senso di un vita vissuta minuto per minuto, senza pensiero del futuro, senza ombra di tenerezza e di melanconia. Sorelle, quando ce n'era, di una prestanza fisica insolente, giovani che avevano scelto un destino corto e intenso e dichiaravano di non curarsi affatto della seconda memoria degli uomini purché la vita che era loro dato di vivere fosse piacevole e vittoriosa. Fra costoro si reclutavano le grandi sportive, le avventuriere più pericolose, quelle che accumulavano enormi ricchezze e le dissipavano, contente solo di prevalere, per qualsiasi mezzo, sul maggior numero d'uomini che potessero. Erano queste, tuttavia, le sole che conservassero un umor chiaro, accostabile, e si lasciassero parlar d'amore, e magari di nozze, con una certa condiscendenza: anche se i loro matrimoni eran di corta durata e tempestosi, macchiati persino da strane dicerie, come quella che le accusava di succhiare, nottetempo, il sangue dei mariti addormentati. A parte simili favole, dilaganti in un mondo troppo familiarizzato coll'invisibile, e perciò esposto a ogni maniera di insidie, nelle unioni non si tentava neppure di estinguere un tacito malinteso iniziale, mancandovi totalmente ogni segno di amicizia e di carità, ugualmente inutile a un uomo garantito contro la morte e alla sua effimera compagna. Divampate con straordinaria e quasi disperata violenza, le passioni si spengevano rapidamente e capricciosamente. Non avevano più senso e calore neppure d'illusione fuggitiva le solite frasi degli amanti: « in eterno », « fino alla morte ». L'uomo che, trascinato dalla foga e dall'abitudine del vecchio linguaggio amoroso, si abbandonasse a simili espressioni, non le pronunziava che a mezza voce e smozzicate, avvertendo nel proprio accento un sapore d'incredula leggerezza: e la donna, per cui avrebbero avuto un senso così drammatico, se ne asteneva rigorosamente, mentre, ascoltandole, o fingeva di non avere inteso, o rimaneva per qualche minuto sospesa e accigliata. Si procreava ancora: ma i mesi della gravidanza erano periodi d'infernale trepidazione, talché era penetrato nel costume l'uso, per i futuri padri, di assentarsi dalle case e non ritornarci che a parto avvenuto. Il presentimento della maternità opprimeva infatti l'incinta, divisa fra il desiderio di partorire il maschio privilegiato che le verrebbe da lontani tempi e per altri tempi ripartirebbe, e il terrore di portare in seno il destino di una nuova infelice, una femminuccia diseredata. Quando l'infante compariva, sembrava — cosa nuova e disumana — che nella madre esausta e appagata risorgesse la donna che invidiava al figlio la sorte di esser uomo. Nascendo una bambina eran poi sospiri lacrime, e, intorno al letto, condoglianze appena velate di rassegnazione, come per un lutto previsto: mentre la puerpera si prodigava alla fantolina con una tetra esclusiva passione.

A tutto si fa l'abitudine, e gli uomini trovarono compenso alle crudezze e ai rancorosi sbalzi di una vita domestica di cui si dichiaravano incolpevoli (la introspezione, in loro stava riducendosi alla semplicità più elementare), riaffidandosi ai più vieti pregiudizi sul poco cervello delle donne, il loro umore illogico, la loro debole resistenza nervosa. Che colpa avevano essi, dopo tutto, se eran stati chiamati a goder per primi, e forse soli, una nuova sorte benevola? Parliamoci chiaro, era meschino e puerile, alla fine, questo ostinarsi a pretendere ciò che la natura negava, e sempre s'è saputo che un uomo non è fatto come una donna. Chissà, gli antichissimi popoli, colle loro leggi tutte virili, non presentissero questa nascosta ragione della superiorità dell'uomo. Non s'eran contentati tutti, del resto, fino a pochi anni innanzi, di vivere una volta sola? Come si giustificano tutte queste smanie? Via, via, non ce lo ha poi assicurato il Padreterno in persona che si rinasce, scherzava un buontempone, il più orgoglioso, forse, fra quanti ebbero il privilegio della seconda memoria. E un altro che, d'indole più tenera, avrebbe voluto confortare quelle poverette che gli facevano pena, a beneficio, magari, di una sorella già vicina ai trenta e nubile, lo faceva, malgrado le sue inclinazioni, con una goffaggine sbrigativa che troppo sapeva di sforzo ostentato.

L'uomo, insomma, non era più umano da quando si sapeva immortale: l'interesse medesimo per la conservazione della famiglia e della specie era squalificato dalla riflessione che ormai non si moriva che per poco. Alla peggio sei secoli, un millennio: il tempo di riposarsi. Nuovi e fortunati spunti per la letteratura amena, per i frizzi degli attori comici scaturivano dalla casuistica del rinascer più presto o più tardi. Ma più grave, insieme grottesca e spietata, appariva l'alterazione dei costumi quando la morte presentava le sue immutate anche se temporanee scadenze. Il sentimento dei moribondi nel progressivo mancar dello spirito vitale era pur sempre di un definitivo sgomento dinanzi a cui le assicurazioni della seconda memoria risultavano tutt'altro che probanti: ma, fra i parenti e gli amici, gli uomini non erano affatto disposti, anche per egoistici riflessi, a concedere, a tollerare debolezze. L'abbattimento del morente, era appena compatito come una fase prevista di una malattia benevola. Col pretesto di distoglierlo dalle sofferenze e di dimostrargli che si era sicuri della sua sorte avvenire, si parlava, intorno al suo letto, gagliardamente e quasi lietamente di quella specie di viaggio, di quell'operazione onerosa sì, ma di sicuro esito. Ilari eran gli ultimi saluti di chi rimaneva in vita, sorridenti le promesse di ritrovarsi presto, di riconoscersi, mentre non era da escludere, fra i più giovani assistenti a quelle morti, la speranza che, col progredire degli studi, si arrivasse a scavalcare questa spiacevole formalità e si potesse dunque durare eterni, così come ci si trovava, senza la noia di rinascere. Soltanto le donne di casa, richiamate, qualunque fosse il loro precedente contegno, all'ufficio di infermiere, non sapevano trattenere le lacrime: mostrandole anzi, apertamente, anche al moribondo. Per loro sole, infatti, la perdita era definitiva, in ognuno che morisse esse morivano, e per sempre. Riprese acerbamente per questa mancanza di logica che turbava l'agonizzante (« nemmeno se morisse una donna! ») non rimaneva loro che nascondersi per abbandonarsi a un pianto in cui la disperazione di sé prevaleva, legando ogni moto d'affetto e barbaramente opprimendo l'animo. Tanto più inselvatichivano. E in questi segreti supplizi venendo a risuonare al loro orecchio il rintocco delle campane d'altri secoli, bizzarria anacronistica risuscitata dalle « Sorelle del ricordo » per segnare occupazioni comuni, le avresti vedute alzare istintivamente al cielo un viso che a poco a poco s'incantava d'una disperata serenità. Della morte, poi, delle donne, si evitava persin di parlare, convenendo tutti nella opportunità di risparmiarsi il contagio della tristezza, morbo inutile e superato, debellato insieme alla morte. Si narravano tuttavia, con uno stupore misto di scetticismo, rari episodi in cui una inalterabile umanissima tenerezza pretendeva trionfare della più ovvia realtà. Si videro mariti che, sul proprio letto di morte, stringevano la mano della consorte sbigottita, e fino all'ultimo respiro le promettevano, come ne avessero avuto rivelazione certissima, il prossimo riscatto del genere femminile e un nuova vita insieme: mentre le mogli mostravano eroicamente di crederli e riuscivano a sorridere. Successe anche che a qualche donna, sul punto di trapassare, venne offerta, per pietoso viatico, la notizia che, poniamo, nel Sudafrica le ragazze cominciavano a « ricordare » davvero. Ma, si è detto, eran casi eccezionali, generose curiosità. Intorno al letto delle moribonde il lutto ebbe un carattere di desolazione mai conosciuta: tanto potente da paralizzare anche il tentativo d'illudere la paziente sulle sue condizioni. Il clima di quelle stanze era così difficile da sopportare, che era scusato e giustificato chi se ne discostava per non ritornare che a seppellimento avvenuto. Va notato che solo in una circostanza il destino dei due sessi concordava, ed era quella dei funerali. Coll'andar degli anni agli uomini ripugnò sempre di più il costume dei cimiteri, questa testimonianza effimera di un ricordo che non aveva più senso: delle salme ci si sbarazzava in mille modi, definitivi e meccanici. Alle donne si lasciò la libertà delle tombe, se ci tenessero. Risultò che, nella maggioranza, le rifiutavano, forse aborrendo da un segno così tangibile della loro sorte immutata. Si diceva che fra le mura dei collegi vigessero associazioni funerarie che disponevano di tombe speciali e le curavano, ma per la verità, non ne appariva segno, tanto che si favoleggiò di catacombe segrete, visitate nottetempo e onorate con funzioni di suffragio da secoli neglette. In sostanza rimaneva l'impressione che morti e morte scomparissero allo stesso modo, senza lasciar traccia. Quanto ai gusti e alle espressioni della vita, ogni anno diveniva più chiaro che delle donne, del loro spirito e anche della loro compagnia, gli uomini facevan sempre meglio a meno; e le donne degli uomini, come succede ai disgraziati che non trovano la naturalezza e la confidenza se non fra loro.

Sciolte dunque, nella migliore e maggior parte, dai legami di famiglia, contagiate di morte fin dalla nascita, esse arrivarono gradualmente e concepire nella esistenza in comune una difesa e anche la libertà di consegnarsi ognuna al proprio istinto, alla propria inclinazione naturale. Nel 2700, infatti, s'inizia la prima generazione di quelle grandi poetesse che, a tutt'oggi, si ammirano alla pari col leggendario Omero. Una mano misteriosamente felice nella scelta dei suoni e del colori, una incomparabile velocità di espressione, una nuova arte della parola, insomma, distingue le loro opere e lo stesso senso della poesia ebbe da loro suggello e nome come in tempi remoti era avvenuto per le imprese dell'ago e del ricamo. Disattenti e dediti a un culto dell'azione sempre più imperioso, gli uomini se ne disinteressavano, negando a quell'attività le lodi di pazienza e gentilezza che pure eran toccate alle casalinghe. Forse agiva in loro un istinto di difesa, di diffidenza, di imbarazzo. Ma eran principalmente le loro compagne, quelle che rimanevano nelle loro case, a farsene beffe: quando, addirittura, non se ne impaurivano. In queste, l'inferiorità del destino aveva generato infinite superstizioni e, per esempio, il convincimento che l'esistenza delle comunità femminili fosse una maledetta macchia che le pregiudicava e di cui non arriverebbero mai a lavarsi, malgrado ogni studio di rendersi piacevoli, allegre, prolifiche. Nouvi costumi si erano andati formando, la fedeltà della donna si rivolgeva più all'uomo che al compagno, talché essa veniva ripresa assai più severamente per sospetto di simpatia verso le sorelle isolate che per concedersi a più d'uno. Purché la prole maschile fosse numerosa, poco si curava la paternità. Ormai le madri di femmine, compatite e vergognose, non cessavano d'inveire contro l'indulgenza degli stati che dimenticavano le comunità anzi le lasciavano, per superba indifferenza, moltiplicare liberamente; a danno, dicevano, delle loro disgraziate figliole che un giorno ne sarebbero attratte. Loro, invece, non se ne dimenticavano mai; e in tutt'altra maniera da questa, aspra e rancorosa, se ne rammentavano quand'erano malate e abbandonate dai medici: i quali, per logica di cose, badavano ormai più a estirpare il dolore che a guarire le malattie. In segreto e tremando, mandavano allora a chiamare certe medichesse delle isolate, celebri per cure pazienti e prodigiose. Salvate, spesso avveniva che nel raccoglimento e nella fievolezza della convalescenza, rimanessero prese nella rete di una immensa gratitudine che le conduceva poi, passo passo, sulla soglia delle dimore precluse. Di rado le varcavano, ma pur qualcuna si faceva coraggio e chiedeva d'essere accolta: rimanendo poi sbigottita da un clima che le riusciva più triste della morte che aveva evitata. E davvero la qualità del silenzio e dei brevi esili suoni che componevano il linguaggio fra quelle mura, eran tali da atterrire la transfuga e ricondurla alla vita agitata e pesante degli uomini.

Erano, nelle comunità, casi previsti e scusati. D'altronde pareva naturale che gli uomini, padroni di molte vite, non ricorressero alle evasioni e ai recuperi dell'arte e schivassero il regime di quiete e di solitudine necessario a favorirla. Sapersi abbandonate e perse nell'eternità come relitti e chiuder gli occhi per inventare un'altra vita, era stata tragedia e, subito, scoperta. Una scoperta vecchia quanto il mondo, ma che le donne avevan ritrovato per conto loro, riproponendosi intensamente ogni antico problema umano. Avidamente innamorate del loro breve soggiorno terreno, facevan tesoro di ogni attimo, prolungandolo in echi tanto profondi quanto parsimoniosi: quasi temessero di consumare un corto respiro in futili fatiche, massaie dell'ispirazione. E mentre, per le ragioni di un costume quasi claustrale, le loro esperienze si rarefacevano in quantità, i loro strumenti di espressione divenivano sempre più delicati e prensili, sicché per ogni minuta sensazione il suono e il segno si differenziavano, articolati e lievi come ombre sull'acqua. I sentimenti, troppo brutali per quel linguaggio, eran tutti trasferiti in simboli da cui traluceva un affetto rigoroso e casto, dardeggiato dalla certezza della morte, fine comune, abbraccio comune. Le cose vedute, una foglia, un sasso, senza posa rinnovate dalla potenza di un occhio implacabilmente acuto, diventavano i cristalli dai mille riflessi, inconsunti e segreti che l'infanzia scopre in un vetro colorato. Era mirabile come alla cautela sapiente dei loro mezzi poetici si accoppiasse una straordinaria innocenza di riflessi: questa innocenza si riscontrava anche nella vita pratica di quei cenobi, anzi andava propagandovisi come una malattia, talché, malgrado le condizioni biologiche e di medicina vi fossero studiate e approfondite, poteva prevedersi il tempo in cui quella particolare umanità vivrebbe in perpetua meraviglia ed ignoranza degli istinti vitali.

E finalmente anche la musica, tanto aliena allo spirito inventivo delle donne, si concesse loro per intero, esse la formarono e composero in nuovi modi, dopo averla per millenni coltivata da esecutrici soltanto. Le loro armonie si svolgevano per movimenti d'una nitidezza incrinata, archi lievi di suono sotto cui il silenzio rimaneva attivo come la calotta di un cielo notturno con cui la fantasia infantile si confronti. Le case delle comunità ne erano come avvolte, e difficilmente i nervi degli uomini potevano sopportarle. È nota e addirittura proverbiale la temerarietà a cui essi si abbandonavano in quei tempi di trapasso, tutti spesi in una quotidiana scommessa e in rischi gratuiti che alimentavano competizioni estreme e guerre, come si sa, caotiche. Nulla c'era da perdere perché tutto era guadagnato, assicurato in anticipo. E se esisteva chi ancora coltivasse un naturale desiderio di raccoglimento e di meditazione, veniva deriso dai più, anzi disprezzato come indegno del titolo di uomo, dunque d'immortale. Si ragionava che a un'umanità riscattata dalla morte non conveniva più un'arte tutta impressa dal sentimento della caducità: che bisognava attendere nuove ere felici con esse il frutto splendido di una nuova poesia. Questo secolo della Grande Scoperta vuol essere celebrato senza debolezze nostalgiche e coll'animo degli Eroi. La vecchia arte è triste, lasciamo che le povere donne ne intossichino i loro anni brevi. Dopo il Tempo, si conquisti lo Spazio, l'Universo. Come si vede, anche il linguaggio degli uomini assumeva caratteri particolari, ma di conformismo a una retorica quasi militaresca che non si limitava, purtroppo, alle forme di espressione, modellando anzi il contenuto del pensiero e del sentimento. Erano a fatica tollerati quei ragazzi che, fra in quindici e i vent'anni, mostravano interesse per i vecchi miti e magari scrivevano versi e dipingevano. Tali fenomeni venivano spiegati con un ritardo di sviluppo e cioè del manifestarsi della memoria anteriore. C'era poi sempre di mezzo un amoretto platonico con una ragazza allevata nelle comunità, cose che gli uomini fatti non prendevano sul serio. Soltanto le madri, con quel loro odio inguaribile per le compagne isolate, davano in ismanie chiamando la fanciulla strega e maliarda. Ma dovevano presto rassicurarsi perché l'assurdo colloquio finiva in monologo e le arti cineree della povera ammaliatrice sortivano un effetto d'incanto breve che nel tumulto della immancabile rivelazione svaniva come in fondo a un'acqua densa. Nel migliore degli incontri le toccava subire la pietà, sul terreno infido delle evasione, delle messe promesse, delle riserve mentali. « Addio » diceva la giovane: mentre la gentilezza malviva del fugace cavaliere mentiva un « arrivederci » di convenienza.

Il genere umano, insomma, s'era spaccato a metà come una mela. Al principio del nuovo secolo gli uomini cominciarono a provare per lo spirito femminile una sorta di ribrezzo; essi tentavano di superarlo ricorrendo a contatti elementari con femmine mentalmente poco sviluppate che formavano l'esercito sempre più grosso delle donne di piacere, mentre il rifiuto delle nozze era adesso eguale nei due sessi e l'istituto familiare una reliquia. Con processi speciali queste donne, diligentemente scelte e preparate, si rendevano attive procreatrici e i medici assicuravano che tanto bastava a fronteggiare il pericolo degli scarsissimi matrimoni, ostacolo, coll'andar del tempo, alle future rinascite. È da notarsi che nell'ottimismo monotono di quella società senza poeti, gli storici resistevano. Ma erano storici singolari, che provvisti di mezzi di ricerca eccezionali, ultima parola del metodo scientifico, raggiungevano tuttavia risultati privi di mordente e soltanto riferiti alla conclusione monotona che tanto i casi degli individui più geniali, come le vicende delle civiltà più fulgide, non rappresentavano che materia grezza e, per così dire, alimento e concime alla maturazione del prodigio dal cervello degli uomini partorito nella moderna età, spontaneamente. In forma di dogma, questa persuasione galleggiava su un mare di cronaca minuta degli antichi e antichissimi secoli: una miriade di segnali, si sarebbe detto, a cui i viventi si aggrappavano per riconoscersi e per consolidarsi nella situazione di posteri eterni. Pochi e industrializzati narratori lavoravano su questi motivi, mettendo insieme massicci romanzi a intreccio plurisecolare, assai bene accetti ai lettori che erano in prevalenza lettrici, e cioè le casuali compagne degli uomini, sempre pronte, almeno in apparenza, a venerare le fortune virili e a tradirle per un attimo di piacere, ossia di infima libertà. Sui primi anni del '700, ogni interesse parve poi riassorbito nell'attesa frenetica dell'avvenimento che doveva convalidare la ancor vibrante conquista: dico il primo rincarnarsi di chi era morto dopo il '617. Ché: più d'un secolo, pareva l'umanità avesse deciso di non pazientare per una definitiva conferma del suo privilegio.

E fu proprio nell'estate '710, calda, a quanto narrano, più dell'ordinario, che in un ritiro della « Universal Women Soul », esattamente nella circoscrizione di Valloria, Agnese Grasti, musicista trentenne, ebbe una strana mattinata. Sedeva al piano cercando una soluzione di nesso fra due episodi di una sua partitura, quando oppressa, come le parve, dall'afa, si lasciò distrarre da uno spontaneo movimento delle dita che ritrovavano, senza ragione apparente, il dettato di un antichissimo adagio. Pensò di aver letto quella pagina nella prima gioventù, da scolaretta, e si meravigliò vagamente di riconoscerla con una ricchezza di consenso e di suggestione a cui non trovava, nei ricordi, riscontro. A misura che, docilissimo, il dettato si sdipanava, l'animo veniva avviato a una specie di gratitudine arcana a cui si univa, causa od effetto, un ineffabile alleggerimento della coscienza, non disgiunto da un fisico tremore, quasi anche il corpo stesse perdendo il necessario peso. Con una precisa scossa questo stato di grazia urtò alla fine in qualcosa di troppo solido, ed era il crescere di una luce torrenziale che, invadendo da una sorgente ignota e tutta interiore, forzava la possibilità d'intendere e di vedere. In questa luce Agnese si sentì d'un tratto fermata e ritta, colla propria ombra ai piedi, un'ombra che non le somigliava, ma la inchiodava a un esatto riconoscersi, mentre altre ombre ne nascevano, spuntando come germogli primaverili dalla terra. Erano oggetti e persone, e un vento, e un gonfior di nuvole memorabili, mentre lo spazio si proiettava a riceverli, tuonando dolcemente in profondità. E già il palato vibrava toccando sillabe ritrovate, ma la donna sbigottita era balzata in piedi, mentre il coperchio della tastiera, ribattuto con violenza, svegliava in allarme tutte le corde dello strumento.

Nelle carte che essa lasciò a un'amica sotto la clausola di non divulgarle prima che un cinquantennio non fosse trascorso, questi ed altri momenti della sua straordinaria e purtroppo estrema avventura possono seguirsi sempre più rilevati da un dubbio che aveva, già nascendo, tutta l'amarezza del sospetto. Dagli anni di un'infanzia fin di secolo, colma di leggende già scontate sul privilegio degli uomini, e di esempi su quel che valesse, s'era avvezzata a soffrire, ma non come esclusa. Dividersi dal padre e dai fratelli le era costato, a disprezzarli, per la commune sordità del sesso, non s'era risolta e da lontano continuava ad amarli. Ma nel momento che — non poteva dubitarne — si sentì chiamata alla stessa loro sorte, forse iniziatrice, anche per le compagne, di un nuovo e simile destino, il suo giudizio si scatenò, mentre l'animo faticava a superare le istigazioni dell'istinto, tripudiante, bisogna pur dirlo, della speranza che aveva perduto gli uomini. Essi erano stati colti alla sprovvista, suggeriva maliziosamente questo istinto, non avevano saputo custodire i loro beni. Affinate dalle sofferenze, noi feconderemo invece l'infinità del tempo coi frutti di un lungo travaglio e porteremo l'umanità a uno stato di angelica esultanza. « Ecco quali retoriche aberrazioni bussano al mio cervello » scriveva Agnese annotando scrupolosamente i suoi pensieri « Fino a quanto potrò dominarmi e dominarlo? »

Sembra accertato che dall'istituto che la ospitava essa si allontanò la sera stessa: trasferendosi, come poi si seppe, in un albergo della città di terraferma dove le isolate non avevano sedi: perché anche i centri abitati seguendo i costumi di chi ci viveva, s'eran divisi in due parti ben distinte e in certo modo difese l'una dall'altra, come ghetti. Non sapremo mai se fosse il suo eccezionale tormento a insinuarle il pensiero di una trepidazione insolita nel contegno delle compagne che la videro uscire. « Hanno capito » scriveva più tardi nella sua camera occasionale « hanno indovinato dal mio aspetto che io avevo in mano la loro sorte. La voce di Gemma era tremante nel salutarmi, Costanza non mi ha mai guardata con tanta insistenza: e perché mai stridevano così forte le ragazze nella sala di studio? » E il giorno dopo le viene in mente che qualcun'altra stia passando la stessa prova, qualcuna che non abbia la forza di tacere e di riflettere. « A quest'ora la notizia si è diffusa, e la mia condotta interpretata come una fugo allo sbaraglio, un addio alla esistenza che insieme abbiamo costruita ».

Della settimana che Agnese Grasti passò lontana dalla comunità, un preciso diario registra la cronaca: una cronaca più interiore che esterna, ma in cui l'esame del proprio caso personale, e l'urgere di quella seconda memoria che tanto aveva straniati Mariano Pietrangeli e i suoi contemporanei, cedevano sempre più visibilmente a un senso di responsabilità e, quasi, di colpa. Deve esser stato, il suo, una specie di ritiro diabolico, dacché non risulta che Agnese uscisse mai dalla sua stanza d'albergo. La stagione torrida aveva d'altronde spopolata quella parte della città abitualmente tanto rumorosa e gaudente, solo il cielo era fitto di alianti che cercavano un refrigerio alla calura. Seguendo collo sguardo quell'aerea moltitudine e riportandolo all'orizzonte sulle rovine di Venezia, immote e brillanti sotto il sole: « o benedetti voi » pensava la donna « morti senza sospetto di rivivere, incalzati da un tempo ancora insondabile e clemente ». Il silenzio, intorno, era tetra presenza, dura a sopportarsi, come il più cupo frastuono. Gli altissimi e lisci blocchi degli edifici di Valloria, abbacinavano; incandescenti e deserti, privi di finestre e di verde: così li vedeva Agnese, nello specchio del mirino di cui ogni stanza era provvista; perché gli uomini avevano da tempo rinunziato alle antiche finestre e terrazze, ancora usate dalle comunità. Di tanto in tanto, sordi boati attestavano l'esistenza di macchine potenti, quelle che provvedevano aria e luce all'edificio, e che Agnese conosceva soltanto per fama; essa non sapeva bene se la sua stanza si trovasse all'ultimo piano o nelle profondità della terra, le costruzioni avevano radici profondissime nel suolo, il moto degli ascensori essendo indifferenziato tanto per la salita come per la discesa. Prigioniera volontaria, venne il momento che Agnese respinse il mirino da cui i quattro punti cardinali di una terra brulla accorrevano magicamente al suo comando, per abbandonarsi a una nostalgia con cui i palpiti della sua nuova coscienza coincidevano. Seconda memoria e vita della comunità formavano un unico rimpianto, e il trovarsi chiusa in quella scatola dall'aria di montagna divenne la prova che né l'una né l'altra potevano raggiungersi senza un atto capitale e definitivo.

« Per questi riflessi, a cui non mancava la logica » scrive l'amica depositaria del suo segreto, intervenendo con una pura relazione dei fatti « dovette maturare una decisione della cui efficienza e rettitudine temo che nessuno riescirà mai giudice imparziale. Rammento benissimo che, in effetti, le abitatrici della nostra comunità passarono, durante quei giorni, un periodo di depressione nervosa tutto particolare, e che se ne dette la colpa al caldo eccessivo. Quanto a me, ricordo che l'assenza di Agnese mi teneva stranamente agitata, incapace di distinguere le cause di una inquietudine così eccezionale. Ma quando la vedemmo tornare, verso sera, se qualcuna la trovò pallida, tutte la sentirono tranquilla. Quel gran caldo s'era sciolto, nel pomeriggio, in un temporale violentissimo che, d'un colpo, aveva mutato la stagione, eravamo contente di aver freddo e ci parve un gaio miracolo accendere così presto le lampade. La notte ci portò un gran riposo, come se da settimane non avessimo dormito: le ragazze si addormentarono dopo essersi raccontate lunghe favole sugli inverni antichi, quando per scaldarsi si bruciava la legna e il carbone e il fumo saliva al cielo, grigio come le nuvole di quella sera. Fra il sonno, sentivamo ancora tuonare, e sciacquare le onde della laguna contro il muro del giardino. Qualcuna affermò poi di aver inteso il suono dello strumento di Agnese e di esserne stata felice, come se quelle armonie straordinarie ci proteggessero contro la tempesta. Io non le udii, purtroppo ».

Pare che Agnese si sia uccisa trattenendo il respiro, fino a che il cuore le scoppiò, come una eroina antica. « Le levai dalle fredde mani queste carte credendole di musica e mi stupii trovandoci parole in luogo di pentagrammi. Fino all'ultimo, così, ci parlò, e non a noi soltanto. Essa si rivolgeva agli uomini e li chiamava fratelli. Dopo i nuovi avvenimenti che parrebbero infirmare la validità della seconda memoria, siamo in grado d'intendere quanto avesse ragione ».

Si rizzò sulle staffe, a un palmo dalla sella, il magro cavaliere: busto eretto, gambe rigidamente tese. Non portava elmo, gli copriva il capo un turbante di leggera seta bianca: la destra sollevata all fronte gli riparava gli occhi dal riverbero: una mano molto piccola che si perdeva nel largo guanto di cuoio grezzo. Aveva guance scavate e imberbi di un pallor livido, tutto il suo aspetto denunciava una contristata giovinezza, tuttavia, guardandolo di sotto in su, il selvatico mandriano che rispondeva: Non so, non avrebbe saputo dargli un'età e neanche decidere se fosse un legato mussulmano in missione presso i crociati o un cavaliere franco della seconda generazione, di quelli che adottano il costume orientale. Lo seguiva uno scudiero biondo, bianco, gigantesco, montato su un cavallone grigio, dalle enormi zampe frangiate di pelo. I due si erano fermati sul ciglio di una larga vallata che digradava in forma di conca, priva affatto di vegetazione e coperta di un giallo fango secco fittamente screpolato. Nel punto più basso della conca stagnava un fondiccio di acqua melmosa: forse quanto rimaneva di una viva sorgente o di un ameno laghetto.

Dopo un lungo minuto di contemplazione, il cavaliere lasciò ricadere la mano e si volse con un piglio così minaccioso che quegli a cui era diretto (un vecchietto di pelo rado e mento aguzzo che, su un cavalluccio smilzo stava per affacciarsi alla vallata) cominciò a mugolare scuse non richieste. Per Allah, diceva non ti ho ingannata, questo è proprio il luogo dove Timurtash teneva le sue donne e te, fra loro, come ostaggio cristiano. Vent'anni fa la terra era verde e il lago azzurro, un paradiso, ma da allora la guerra ha succhiato le vene del suolo, erba e alberi sono morti sotto le zampe dei cavalli: e l'aria è avvelenata.

Ma il magro cavaliere non parve ascoltarlo e neppure si curò di essere stato riconosciuto come donna e come persona. Aveva chiuso gli occhi per fermare dietro le palpebre le immagini che la realtà smentiva fulminandole con la luce impietosa di un torrido sole. Soffocata dall'afa, continuava a vedere la collina boscosa, il ruscello, il lago dove gaie ragazze si tuffavano, nuotavano sott'acqua spruzzandosi di gocce iridescenti per poi approdare sul prato e lì giocare avvinghiate in una lotta da cui si scioglievano stremate e languide: persino il vento infocata si mutò, per un lungo istante, in un fresco alito silvestre. Fu l'ardore della gola a risvegliarla da una così intensa illusione: riprese le redini nelle piccole mani guantate, l'amazzone volse le spalle alla conca e via dirupò per il terreno franoso che poco innanzi aveva penosamente salito. Imbarazzato dal peso del proprio corpo lo scudiero normanno faticava a impedire che le zampe della sua bestia affondassero nel pietrisco. Quanto al vecchietto lamentoso aveva smesso di gemere, era lui adesso che precedeva il terzetto, favorito dalla cavalcatura leggera che quasi volava. Arrivato per primo in fondo al dirupo, si fermò e, raggiunto dai compagni, chiese con laconica autorità: Dove volete pernottare stasera? Il rifugio migliore è lontano, i vostri cavalli sono stanchi e hanno sete. Vi converrà accomodarvi sotto quelle rocce laggiù prima che il sole tramonti, lì c'è un pozzo non ancora disseccato.

Senza attendere un consenso spronò il cavallino e si avviò, non senza aver prima sogguardato di tralice il finto cavaliere. La conosceva benissimo, sebbene lei non lo sospettasse: più volte l'aveva vista ad Antiochia,[1] nel cerchio della principessa Costanza, erede dello Stato. Sapeva che era sorella della superba Alice, come lei figlia di re, ma ancor nubile per non aver trovato un uomo degno della sua nascita disposto a sposarla: cosa naturale, giacché gli uomini, principi o borghesi, amano le donne formose e costei è tutta pelle e ossa. Portava già panni virili quando l'aveva fatto chiamare come guida esperta del territorio di Sheiraz,[2] e lui aveva accettato senza batter ciglio, fissando un prezzo esoso. Avendo intuito lo scopo del viaggio e preveduto la delusione che ne sarebbe seguita, aveva poco fa temuto che lo scudiero biondo gli usasse

---

[1]Una città nelle Siria antica, una principalità fondata dai Cristiani sulla terra occupata dai Mussulmani nel 1098 durante la Prima Crociata.

[2]Sheiraz: una città nel centro-sud dell'Iran.

violenza. Gli dà noia, adesso che quei due gli siano alle spalle; meglio farsi di lato cedere il passo alla principessa che viene avanti tetra, le spalle curve, il busto rilassato, i grandi occhi persi verso l'arido orizzonte. Stolta ragazza. Perché non se n'è stata quieta, presso i suoi illustri parenti, nella regina delle città, la bella, ricca, frequentata Antiochia, ove non era escluso che un baronello povero e ambizioso sperasse una fortuna dalle nozze con una donna regale? Ma già: questa Joveta — ne sa anche il nome — ha da bambina gustato la dolcezza del costume mussulmano e non può dimenticarla sebbene i Franchi, in tutti questi anni di conquista, si siano addomesticati. Una cosa è vivere fra le ragazze dell'harem, spensierate, sicure della protezione del loro signore; un'altra passar mesi e mesi chiusa fra le mura di un castello arcigno, esposta agli assedi, con l'unico passatempo della rocca, del telaio e delle pratiche di una religione crudele: come se ad Allah giungessero le preghiere delle donne.

Al silenzio della terra risponde il silenzio dei tre viaggiatori. Nessuno parla. Il vecchio mussulmano per disprezzo degli infedeli, lo scudiero per l'incapacità di pensare in una lingua sconosciuta, la principessa per l'avvilimento di una situazione senza uscita. Lei, autonoma, scontrosa, autoritaria, anzi capricciosa (suo padre si divertiva alle sue bizze) ridotta a cercarsi un asilo che non somigli all'ospitalità concessa a una parente povera. Del resto, i fatti parlano chiaro: Baldovino[3] non aveva pensato a provvederla di un piccolo feudo, sicuro che non le sarebbe mancato uno sposo. Morto lui, eran cominciate le contese e le ripicche fra Gerusalemme, Tripoli, Edessa, Antiochia, in gara a proporle un marito mediocre per lo più anzianotto, che dapprima si diceva onorato e consentiva a ogni clausola: e a poco a poco s'impuntava, reclamava, ripartiva per il suo paese.

Lunghe giornate, adesso, al riparo umidiccio di una caverna, oppure in fetidi alberghi di cammellieri; rapide notti di marcia sotto il cielo nero ronzante di stelle voraci. M'immagino, disse il vecchio che via via pareva crescere in statura come in insolenza, che vogliate raggiungere la costa e la città di Tripoli: altrove non c'è salvezza per voi né convenienza per me. Che cosa ribattere e come redarguirlo se senza di lui, i due sconsigliati viaggiatori sarebbero morti di fame e di sete? La sua bisaccia, alla vista così leggera, era inesauribile, ogni giorno ne scaturivano focacce, datteri, un otre di acqua freschissima e mai era successo che i cavalli non gradissero i bizzarri foraggi che lui riusciva a inventare. Questo miracoloso potere di sopravvivere suscitava nella principessa un superstizioso rispetto e dovunque il vecchio si fermasse per stendervi il

[3]Baldovino II, di Francia, andò in Palestina con la Prima Crociata (1096). Diventò conte d'Edessa (Urfa, Turchia) e poi re di Gerusalemme nel 1118.

suo tappetino di preghiera, lei rimaneva immobile aspettando in un torpido stupore la fine della sua cantilena. Aveva ormai perduto la facoltà di interrogare, di opporsi al volere altrui e inorridiva prevedendo che, una volta giunta a Tripoli sua sorella Hodierna avrebbe disposto di lei come di una schiava.

Cominciavano i campi coltivati, i giardini protetti da alte mura bianche, dalla cima di una collinetta balenò l'azzurro del mare riportandola al confuso ricordo di quando, infante, insieme alla madre e alle sorelle maggiori, lo vedeva brulicante di vele colorate. Poi, discesa la collina, il mare scomparve dietro le fortificazioni della città, irte di torri. Quasi la terra lo avesse inghiottito, il vecchio era scomparso, toccò a Joveta parlamentare colle scolte che presidiavano la porta, occupatissime a frugare le bisacce dei contandini e i basti degli asini che premevano per entrare con i loro rifornimenti di cibarie. Decisa a tacere la sua identità, chiese soltanto la strada del palazzo comitale che non le fu indicata senza belle e scherni sulla magrezza sua e del suo cavallo. Ridevano tutti, sgherri e villani ma la presenza del colossale scudiero bastò a sgominarli quando mulinando lo spadone e spronando il possente animale egli s'inoltrò tra gli omuncoli: e la strada fu libera e vuota.

Per la verità una viuzza angusta, stretta fra case chiuse e cieche, accavallate l'una sull'altra. Rimbomba sulle pietre scabre il trotto dei due cavalli, dietro le fitte grate dei terrazzini s'indovinano visi di sequestrate curiose mentre Joveta va via via rammentando che insieme alla madre di lì era passata arrivando da Edessa. L'aria marina, sempre più vivace, attutisce il calore del primo pomeriggio, l'ora dell'inevitabile siesta che rende deserte le strade. È un conforto respirare quel soffio gagliardo, quel messaggio di sconfinata libertà.

Di certo anche Hodierna riposava rispettando il costume d'Oltremare e approfittandone per sottrarsi almeno per qualche ora alle spie del geloso marito: fu arduo convincere i soldati di guardia che lo smunto cavaliere tanto arrogante da chiedere un colloquio con la contessa, fosse, nientemeno, una principessa del sangue. Da ultimo, anche su di loro agì l'imponenza dello scudiero e l'espressione del suo viso, da impassibile di venuto minaccioso. Gli era anche tornata la favella dacché aveva ravvisato fra questi uomini un paio di connazionali in grado d'intendere le sue affermazioni condite da vigorose bestemmie.

Hodierna non dormiva e poiché, alle grida delle sentinelle subentrava il confuso vociare di schiavi e serve spedì una donzella a informarsi di quel che accadeva. Costei era appena uscita dalla sala che vi si affacciò, scrollandosi da chi gli metteva le mani addosso il bizzarro personaggio cagione di tanto fracasso. Semisdraiata fra cuscini di diverse misure, la contessa lo squadrò dal capo alle piante con uno sdegno più fittizio che reale, giacché a esser sincera l'episodio la divertiva. Qualcosa le diceva che lo smilzo giovanotto non le era ignoto e non per i tratti del suo viso ricoperto di polvere, ma per certo modo scattante di muoversi e gestire che le era stato familiare. E fu proprio da uno di quei moti, il gettare all'indietro la testa e con la mano scompigliarsi i capelli che scaturì un'immagine femminile, quella della piccola Joveta tanto avara di parole quanto stramba nell'azione. Così non la stupì affatto che portasse brache corazza e spada né che avesse sostituito l'elmo dei cavalieri con il turbante degli infedeli: non minacciava forse, fin da ragazzina di convertirsi all'Islam?

Il gomito affondato nei cuscini, il mento nella destra, Hodierna riflette sul da farsi. Infine, congedate le ancelle, si leva in piedi: la sua voce strascicata, cantilenante è ancora quella di una adolescente leziosa. Poggia le mani sulle spalle della sorella e senze abbracciarla fissa su di lei quei suoi occhi d'argento che trafiggono anche se vogliono accarezzare. Vorrai spiegarmi, spero, perché hai lasciato Antiochia, chi ti ha menato fin qui e a quale scopo mi arrivi in questo misero arnese. Costanza è ricca suo marito è potente, io vivo prigioniera di uno sposo avaro e sospettoso, anche se lo volessi non saprei come sistemarti decentemente. Tripoli, mia cara, è un porticciolo di mercanti avidi, di pescatori, di prostitute, i cavalieri che ci sbarcano se ne allontanano in fretta, diretti a Gerusalemme. La mia corte è povera, indegna di una figlia di re, nostro padre mi ha sacrificata.

Non è cattiva, Hodierna, ma non sa dimenticare la vita brillante che si conduce ad Antiochia: ogni occasione è buona per lamentarsene. Sospira: parlo per il tuo bene, levati codesti stracci, indossa gli abiti del tuo sesso e del tuo grado, poi si penserà a procurarti un imbarco per Jaffa. Batte le mani, ordina che si portino rinfreschi e poi la principessa sua sorella sia condotta al bagno e alle stanze degli ospiti. Credimi, a Gerusalemme un marito finiranno per trovartelo. Se mi dai retta, giuro che non passa un anno e ti trovi contenta, con un bell'uomo al fianco e gravida. A meno che... S'interrompe: voglio mostrarti i miei figlioli, hanno poca salute purtroppo quest'aria è malefica per i bambini specie se maschi. Per fortuna Raimondo è robusto ma per Melisenda non m'illudo, dimagra a vista d'occhio.

A meno che... Cosa intendeva Hodierna con quella frase lasciata sospesa? Rinfrescata, cosparsa di olii profumati Joveta riposa guardando il mare che palpita sotto la luna. Sebbene cerchi di sfuggirla, la risposta è chiara e coincide con un pensiero che spesso l'ha visitata. A meno che tu non decida di entrare in monastero. Da bambina le monache le facevano paura: ma in fondo, cos'è un convento se non un harem senza letto coniugale? Innanzi tutto, lei non sarebbe una suora come le altre, potrebbe imporre la sua volontà, inventare una nuova regola, esigere una dimora di suo gusto, alleggerire il peso delle incessanti preghiere, dei digiuni, delle mortificazioni. Una specie di compromesso fra la vita dell'harem e quella di un monastero popolato di giovani vivaci, non è poi irrealizzabile. Sua sorella, regina di Gerusalemme, la contenterà assegnandole una dimora amena fra giardini, boschi, acque vive, fontane. Nessuna autorità religiosa o laica le negherà la ricreazione del bagno, delle merende sull'erba, dei giochi e del canto al suono del liuto. Le vesti saranno nitide, graziose: via le lane grigie, le cuffie rigide, saranno permesse le chiome lunghe coperte da un velo. Si pregherà lietamente, senza pensare alla morte.

Un programma così rivoluzionario occupò a tal punto Joveta che essa a stento si accorse di navigare alla volta di Jaffa. Avvisata tempestivamente da Hodierna, la regina l'attendeva e l'accolse con fervide manifestazioni d'affetto. Di carattere dolce e fantasioso amava nella sorella minore l'amica, la complice delle sue follie giovanili, la confidente dei suoi più dolorosi segreti. Non era forse lei, Joveta, che attenta e agile come un capriolo sorvegliava l'ingresso del giardino durante i suoi convegni con Ugo Le Puyset? Dapprima innocenti, poi focosi e straziati, i due amanti si sentivano sicuri quando la bruna giovinetta, ferma a pochi passi di distanza, li proteggeva dal pericolo di essere scoperti. Nessuna sentinella era più discreta, dei baci, degli amplessi pareva non accorgersi: Melisenda sarebbe caduta dalle nuvole se avesse sospettato ciò che Joveta provava all'aspetto, alla voce di Ugo, quanto per ringraziarla la chiamava « mia piccola aquiletta » e le carezzava i capelli.

Ora, abbracciandola, quei tempi lontani tornavano in mente alla regina con tale veemenza che il suo volto, un po' appassito, ma sempre bello, s'inondò di pianto. O cara, cara, singhiozzava e anche le donzelle intorno a lei non trattenevano le lacrime. Quanto a Joveta, a occhi asciutti si sciolse dall'abbraccio e per scendere sulla riva accettò la mano di re Folco[4] che gliela porse con reverenza. Aveva assunto un atteggiamento solenne, quasi ieratico che si addiceva alla sua alta figura, al suo viso angoloso: i marinai, la folla accorsa ammiravano la coppia dei cognati che precedeva la regina. Per la prima volta in vita sua Joveta trionfava, ed era un trionfo che sapeva di vendetta. Ben più violenti di quelli di Melisenda erano i suoi ricordi: il silenzioso amore per Ugo, il suo cupo sacrificio di negletta, infine l'orrore per la tragedia, Ugo pu-

---

[4]Dopo aver visitato la Palestina nel 1120, Folco ci ritornò per sposarsi con Melisenda, la figlia del re Baldovino II di Gerusalemme. Diventò re di Gerusalemme dopo la morte di Baldovino II nel 1131. Durante il primo anno del suo regno risolse una disputa in Antiochia e represse la ribellione organizzata dall'amante di Melisenda, Ugo Le Puiset.

gnalato a morte, mal guarito, scacciato dalla corte per poi agonizzare in solitudine lassù sul Gargano[5] dove l'arcangelo Michele lo aveva chiamato a sè. Questa fine ingloriosa e malinconica era stata per Melisenda un dolore assottigliato dalla distanza, placato dalle pratiche religiose: per Joveta una ferita insanabile, la vera ragione della sua inquieta solitudine. Munita di un tal credito ha ora diritto a un risarcimento che si estenda a tutto il suo futuro: a parlar chiaro la pia Melisenda non potrà negarle nulla.

Ma questo « nulla » cambiò faccia, e a poco a poco si gonfiò di quel che meno ci doveva entrare: non più i privilegi dovuti a una figlia di re che rinunzia al mondo, ma i ben più appetibili diritti di una principessa nubile: una dote cospicua, la signoria di castelli e terre e, soprattutto, un marito. Chi ha sparso la notizia di una sua prossima monacazione? I soliti cortigiani pettegoli, i soliti preti maneggioni. Non passa una settimana e Joveta pretende di essere festeggiata come una sposa con banchetti, danze, tornei. Nomina le sue dame d'onore, sfoggia vesti suntuose: non ha bisogno di chiedere, le basta un'occhiata a Melisenda per esser soddisfatta al di là dei suoi desideri, la regina la ama ma ha paura di lei. Che ne direste, propone, della città di Gerico? È una terra fertilissima e poi

---

[5]Promontorio del Gargano, al nord est di Foggia, dove fu fondato un santuario di San Michele dopo la sua apparizione a un arcivescovo. Un luogo popolare di pellegrinaggio nel medioevo.

ha un così bel nome, proprio adatto al doario di una badessa. Quale badessa? risponde Joveta inarcando le sopracciglia. Io credevo che voleste donarmela, sempre che piaccia al principe che sposerò. Il suo sorriso è altero, aggressivo e Melisenda, interdetta, non sa come replicare ma pensa: trovarlo, il principe.

Joveta ebbe Gerico e, a palazzo, un appartamento fastoso dove i mercanti sciorinavano le primizie dei loro traffici, sete e drappi e profumi: ma non un marito. Re Folco, buonuomo, glielo cercava con la massima diligenza promettendo cariche proficue e onori. Ecco Bernardo Vacher, ecco Riccardo di Domfort, quarantenni ben portanti che da poco han preso la croce, cadetti di gran casa. Joveta temporeggia, scherza, le fa senso dice, la pelle troppo bianca di questi Franchi. Michele di Gargar, principe armeno senza principato, sembra per qualche giorno il preferito ma corre voce che sia legato agli Assassini.[6] In Antiochia un maga le ha predetto che sposerà un saracino, vuole aspettarlo. Intanto la turbano miraggi di nuove fughe verso le grandi città degli infedeli, Damasco, Bagdad e sempre più in là, nelle terre dei mongoli, sino al Katai. Le tempie le bruciano, il sole le accende lunghi brividi dal collo alle reni. Fra poco sarà vecchia, ha compiuto

[6]Un setto mussulmano segreto del Medio-Oriente. Dall'undicesimo al tredicesimo secolo i suoi soci ammazzarano i loro nemici per motivi religiosi e politici.

ventidue anni, bisogna decidersi, anche la pazienza di re Folco ha un limite e Melisenda trema.

Si decise. Chiusa nelle sue stanze congedò dame d'onore donzelle e paggi a ciascuno donando un oggetto prezioso, un gioiello: poi chiese di conferire col patriarca[7] Guglielmo che la provvedesse di un teologo capace d'introdurla nei più ardui misteri della fede cattolica, giacché, riconobbe, la sua educazione cristiana mancava di fondamenti. Dall'alba alla nera notte si protrassero i colloqui della principessa coll'uomo di Dio, un monaco egiziano cultore di Origene,[8] che spesso finivano in discussioni tempestose. Dopo un mese di clausura, dibattiti e digiuni, ecco Joveta nel circolo della regina, in veste di penitente e magra da far paura. Nel silenzio generale, alzando solennemente la destra, dichiarò che aveva scelto il chiostro ed era pronta ad entrarvi.

Il convento fu subito trovato, quello di Sant'Anna a pochi passi dal palazzo reale: ed ebbe in feudo il villaggio di Betania. Le monache, tutte anziane, furono sloggiate e disseminate in una diecina di conventucci minori, la badessa, decrepita, ebbe il buon senso di morire appena Joveta passò da novizia a professa. Eletta a ventiquattro

---

[7]Il titolo dei vescovi di Roma, Constantinopoli, Gerusalemme, Antiochia e Alessandria.

[8]185–254? D.C. Un teologo, erudito e studioso della Bibbia nella chiesa greca bizantina.

anni alla carica abbaziale, dettò le sue condizioni: nessun controllo vescovile e il riconoscimento, da Roma, del titolo di badessa mitrata.

Il caso portò che il fatiscente edificio, subito invaso da muratori e scalpellini lombardi portasse le tracce del suo antico proprietario, tanto nell'architettura come negli ornamenti di marmi policromi e mosaici: certi vecchioni mussulmani, scampati da ragazzi alla conquista crociata, ricordavano che proprio lì dimorava un potente sceicco, signore di Betania, fanatico cultore di frutteti, collezionista di rarità zoologiche, gran cacciatore alla faccia di Allah. Il monastero, beneficiario delle stesse terre, ci trovò il ben d'Iddio: frutta squisita, fiori, selve, acque correnti, fontane e persino una gabbia dove gli indigeni ancora nutrivano un macilento leone, pronipote di quelli che lo sceicco allevava per suo piacere. Tutta la proprietà era circondata da altissime muraglie fortificate, così che nessuno poteva spiare quanto vi avveniva: se Joveta lo avesse voluto, le giovani che da tutta la Palestina accorrevano per cominciare, sotto una badessa tanto prestigiosa, il loro noviziato, avrebbero potuto abbandonarsi liberamente ai giochi in uso fra le ragazze di Sheiraz. Il possesso di Gerico aggiunto a quello di Betania formava una specie di piccolo regno senza obblighi di vassallaggio al sovrano di Gerusalemme.

Senonché, portati a termine i lavori di consolidamento e di ampliamento, posti in opera i rilievi ornamentali, le statue, rinnovati i giardini, ripuliti i boschi e le macchie, disegnati nuovi viali e sentieri, Joveta si annoiò del suo sogno infantile. I vescovi sanno di latino e di greco, lei non ammetteva di esser da meno, una ricca biblioteca raccolta per suo ordine con gran fatica da un benedettino, occupò la sala più vasta del monastero dove la badessa si applicò per lunghe ore su codici e papiri, sotto la guida di famosi maestri, pellegrini al Santo Sepolcro e arabi sapienti: giacché anche dell'arabo essa volle essere padrona. In breve Joveta lesse i testi greci (così l'assicurava l'ateniese che ne constatava i progressi) meglio di Anna Comnena.[9] Quanto al latino, il precettore prescelto fu, per ragioni non chiarite, un Templario di mezza età che le gravi ferite riportate in guerra avevano escluso dalla milizia e restituito agli studi: grande nemico delle donne come la maggior parte dei cavalieri del Tempio. Da bambina, quei colossi corazzati di ferro, col viso sempre nascosto dall'elmo, la spaventavano: tanto più si ostinò nel suo capriccio. A testa nuda e calva, la faccia scoperta solcata da profonde cicatrici, l'aspetto del Templario rivelava sotto una patina di ostentata crudeltà una disperata stanchezza. Il suo latino duro e gutturale tradiva l'origine germanica: la badessa, avvezza al morbido accento dei

---

[9]Nato nel 1083 e morto verso 1148, una storica bizantina e figlia di Alessio Comneno, l'imperatore bizantino. Scrisse un libro sul padre in greco elegante.

messi papali, si divertiva a correggerne la pronunzia, facendosi, da scolara, maestra.

In tutta la Palestina le ragazze che le nobili famiglie squattrinate destinavano al chiostro, seguitavano a chiedere di monacarsi a Betania, luogo privilegiato per le bellezze naturali, per la regola tutt'altro che severa, per il carattere della superiora, giovane, liberale, potente. L'accoglienza era eguale per tutte: appena arrivate, un bagno tiepido, biancheria di lino sottile: lì finivano le loro illusioni di vita facile. I giardini, i boschi, i ruscelli tanto decantati dovevano contentarsi di vederli dalle finestrine delle loro celle: mai una festa, rare le passeggiate. Le aspettavano, invece, i tavoloni e gli sgabelli della biblioteca, le lezioni di austeri maestri, impazienti della loro ignoranza, la presenza continua della badessa, il suo controllo sulla intelligenza e lo zelo di ognuna. Unico svago le funzioni religiose, fastosissime, unico vantaggio l'ora del risveglio per l'uffizio mattutino, più tarda che nei normali conventi. Con la testa piena di fonemi e segni grafici latini greci arabi, molte giovani deperivano, sostenute solo dalla speranza che una volta giudicate idonee nelle diverse discipline, la badessa avrebbe concesso ai loro piedi impigriti i parchi, i giardini appena intraveduti. Il che avvenne, ma nessuna prevedeva che l'aria campestre, i colori, i profumi le avrebbero stordite e quasi private del piacere di goderne. Mani pallide toccarono ma non colsero neppure uno stelo, qualcuna che ardì immergere le dita nell'acqua di una piscina, subito le ritirò, colta da un brivido. Betania infine rimase un sogno mutatosi in incubo, le porte sulla campagna rimasero aperte ma non c'era chi le varcasse: a Joveta stessa, distolta dal suo capriccio di risuscitare Sheiraz, il lussureggiante scenario delle selve che si stendevano sino alle mura di Gerico, riusciva indifferente. Eppure ne era lei la signora; e un principe deve usare il suo feudo. Il modo le fu suggerito dal gregge delle novizie che spontaneamente eran ritornate in biblioteca: Sant'Anna di Betania diverrà da domani un educandato per le figlie dei principi di Oltremare.

La notizia circolò per le corti, ma con scarsi risultati, padri e madri avevano fretta di maritare le loro ragazze non destinate al chiostro, che a dodici o tredici anni si giudicavano mature per il matrimonio: meglio tenersele accanto, in bella vista, che farne delle saccenti che infastidirebbero i mariti con la loro dottrina. Fra quelle che si presentarono, la maggior parte erano brutte, rozze, di debole comprendonio talché dopo qualche settimana di lezioni inutili furon lasciate libere di vagabondare all'aria aperta, a riempirsi la pancia di frutta acerba e anche esposte a cattivi incontri. Qualche scandaletto fu soffocato, di due allieve uscite di nascosto dalla cinta di Betania non si seppe più nulla. Mancando gli ordini della badessa, le culture vennero abbandonate, l'erba cresceva nei viali, le foglie marcivano nel sottobosco, le acque scorrendo, trascinavano terra e sassi a colmare i letti dei torrenti, poi si distendevano in stagni putridi: a Gerico il governatore favoriva traffici immondi. Intanto nella biblioteca deserta, Joveta si cimentava con le difficoltà del mongolo, approfittando di due prigionieri di guerra procuratile dal Templario.

In questa occupazione la trovò la novizia Gerberga la mattina che, dopo aver timidamente bussato senza ottener risposta, osò entrare e porgere alla badessa il messaggio arrivato or ora da Tripoli di Siria: lo aveva recato un marinaio sbarcato il giorno innanzi a Jaffa. Impegnata col calamo a tracciare segni su un foglio di leggerissimo papiro, Joveta prese con la sinistra il rotolo sigillato, ma non lo svolse. Dice, il marinaio, che la risposta è urgente, balbettò Gerberga e la badessa si alzò, si avvicinò alla finestra, sciolse il nastro, ruppe il sigillo. Lo scritto, dettato da Hodierna, recava la sua firma.

« Vostra Reverenza conoscerà i pericoli da cui siamo minacciati: cospirazioni, raggiri, contese fra me e il conte. Mio figlio Raimondo può difendersi ma la piccola Melisenda è debole e malata. A voi l'affido sperando che le vostre cure possano salvarla, ma rassegnata alla volontà divina »: questa la sostanza del messaggio che si chiudeva annunciando l'imminente arrivo della bambina. Non esisteva dopo tutto, a Sant'Anna, un educandato per fanciulle di nobile stirpe?

Dopo due giorni infatti una lettiga con la sua scorta chiedeva l'accesso al convento. Melisenda febbricitante ne venne fuori, anzi ne fu estratta ché non aveva la forza di camminare. Aveva otto anni ma ne mostrava cinque, tuttavia si espresse con grazia per salutare la venerabile zia. La quale, nell'atto di riceverla, non dubitò un istante che le sarebbe morta fra le braccia, così minute erano le sue ossicine e trasparente il suo visuccio, venato di blù alle tempie. Intenerita da tanta fragilità, non ebbe l'animo di passare ad altri quel lieve peso che depose di persona sul letto più morbido che si trovasse a Sant'Anna. La bambina, pur affannando per la febbre, sorrideva, a occhi chiusi stringendo la mano di Joveta. Sorbito il cordiale che le porgevano, li aprì: erano grandi, di un raro violetto, ma non languidi come gli occhi di una moribonda, anzi vivaci, di una gaiezza innocente. Per tutta la notte la badessa la vegliò sicché crebbe nelle suore la convinzione che la piccola non avrebbe veduto il nuovo giorno: mai la badessa si era prestata a tali uffici, a meno che l'agonia di una consorella non richiedesse la sua presenza.

Invece Melisenda sopravvisse, al mattino nipote e zia furono trovate immerse in un profondo sonno: la monaca speziale che aveva in convento funzione di medico, sentenziò che la bimba non era malata, solo gracile e di sangue povero. Comunque la voce che un miracolo fosse avvenuto a Sant'Anna e per merito della badessa, si sparse per Gerusalemme e il monastero ne riacquistò prestigio. Pur alzando scetticamente le spalle Joveta si sentì rianimata da un nuovo interesse per i suoi compiti di superiora e di governatrice. Chiusa la biblioteca, congedati i maestri, si occupò di bonifiche, di construzioni, di abbellimenti. Una ventina di nuove educande chiesero di essere accolte e la badessa decise di alternare la loro applicazione agli studi del latino e del greco con gli esercizi fisici che il feudo permetteva. Il vecchio miraggio di Sheiraz rifioriva, esse gareggiavano nel nuoto, nella corsa, nei giochi della palla e del cerchio: tutte sapevano già cavalcare, al modo delle castellane occidentali. Solo la piccola Melisenda, cresciuta in statura, ma sempre sottile come un giunco, doveva contentarsi di assistere a questi spassi senza parteciparvi: del che Joveta si doleva quasi essa stessa ne fosse privata. Se ne consolava ammirando la bellezza della nipote che già all'inizio dell'adolescenza prometteva di superare quella delle più celebrate principesse d'Oltremare. Senonché il pensiero che pochi anni la separavano dal suo destino di sposa — già Hodierna, da Tripoli, accennava a possibili pretendenti — provocava in lei una specie di amaro stupore. Dunque era vero, il suo cuore creduto sepolto nella tomba di Ugo Le Puyset, grondava di tenerezza per questa ragazzina del suo sangue, un sangue che lei non amava nelle sorelle e in tutti parenti. Non era amore materno il suo, ma un sentimento strano: bisogno di proteggere, di custodire, di comandare, di essere necessaria alla creatura che il caso le aveva affidata. Bisogno di dare, imperiosamente e senza ricambio: che Melisenda la amasse come la gente dice che si amano le madri, non le era mai venuto in mente e chi glielo avesse insinuato l'avrebbe vista corrucciata ed offesa. Ciò non le impediva di rallegrarsi riflettendo che Melisenda continuava ad essere fragile, delicata, facile ad ammalarsi: gli uomini esigono mogli robuste e feconde, non spose angeliche che un soffio di vento porta via.

Poteva dunque succedere che malgrado i maneggi di Hodierna, la fanciulla non trovasse da accasarsi degnamente e, passando gli anni, e spente le ambizioni della madre, fosse lasciata alla pace di Betania che, del resto, per molti segni mostrava di preferire a un destino incerto. Un giorno, sul proprio letto di morte, Joveta avrebbe designato alla sua successione Melisenda, suggellando così l'oscuro legame che univa le loro affinità di temperamento. Affinità immaginarie, ma la badessa ci contava: le pareva per esempio, di avere sempre posseduto la dolcezza, la docilità della nipote, di somigliarle, insomma, nel carattere e nei gusti, almeno quanto ne differiva nell'aspetto.

Ma: ogni giorno una sorpresa, l'agguato di una scoperta. La pelle candida di Melisenda non ha più la trasparenza dell'alabastro ma il granito nitore del marmo greco; le sue forme si arrotondano lievitando, il violetto dell'iride incupisce. Anche la voce sta mutando: da infantilemente squillante è divenuta argentina e, nei passaggi, flautata, morbida. Alla graziosa pigrizia dei suoi movimenti è subentrata una flessuosa agilità, le sue passeggiate si addentrano sempre più a lungo nei boschi: infine una sera, al tramonto Joveta la scorge mentre sul bordo di un laghetto si denuda della tunica e con muto riso di trionfo s'immerge. Un colpo al cuore questa visione di creatura libera dai fantasmi della malattia, della timidezza, del sogno inerte; questa immagine di donna pronta alla gioia di vivere. Non ne farò mai una badessa: è la prima reazione; la seconda è del tutto materna, palpitante, Joveta si precipita spiegando a due mani un ampio asciugatoio. La pazzarella si è bagnata senza pensare alla tosse, alla febbre cui va soggetta se prende freddo. Ora, sporgendosi dall'orlo dell'acqua l'ansiosa zia si china a raccogliere e tergere quel corpo d'avorio, a massaggiarlo coi gesti di una nutrice mussulmana. Melisenda ride, non teme i rimproveri: e chi potrebbe farglieli? Ma da quella sera la badessa è convinta che la nipote non rimarrà a lungo a Betania, che la propria vecchiaia sarà deserta in espiazione di un affetto che ha gli eccessi della passione.

Per punirsi, subito decide che d'ora innanzi Melisenda sarà un'educanda come le altre, negli studi, nelle ricreazioni, negli orari. Nessun privilegio per lei, nessun riguardo giustificato da una salute malferma: sebbene esile infatti il suo aspetto è florido, gli esercizi fisici communi alle compagne le riescono mirabilmente. Nemica dei cilizi la badessa ne ha inventato per sé uno più lacerante di una cintura di chiodi. Se cavalcare è pericoloso, se mescolarsi alla folla di Gerico è sconsigliabile a evitare il contagio di lebbra e di peste, Melisenda sarà la prima a cui Sua Reverenza insegnerà che il timore non si addice alle dame di alto lignaggio: che se è necessario esse debbono affrontare il pericolo, come i loro padri, fratelli, sposi. La nipote, passata a un così diverso regime di vita, obbediva sorridendo. Aveva penetrato il crudele cimento a cui la zia si sottoponeva e lo commentava fra sé con arguzia. Povera badessa, come non aveva capito che lei era contenta del suo stato e il capriccio del bagno non significava desiderio di mutarlo? Le passeggiate nei boschi, le danze in cerchio con le compagne, qualche bella canzone cantata in coro: altri svaghi non chiedeva e meno che meno uscire dal monastero per ritornare accanto a una madre stravagante, a un fratello dai modi brutali. Con l'età aveva acquistato una facilità di parola e una sicurezza che usò per far rispettosamente intendere a Joveta quali fossero i suoi gusti e le sue scelte. Non ci riuscì, la zia non credeva che a se stessa, alla sua morale di monaca pessimista, autoflagellatrice: tuttavia il suo umore alquanto rischiarato dimostrò che, magari inconsciamente, la antica speranza rigermogliava nel suo animo inaridito. Del resto la scadenza era prossima, fra poco Melisenda compirebbe i quindici anni, età oltre la quale i parenti delle damigelle d'Oltremare stringevano i tempi per il loro accasamento.

Taceva, invece, la corte di Tripoli, quasi immemore delle vantaggiose alleanze che avrebbe potuto concludere attraverso Melisenda. Joveta, dal canto suo, si guardava bene dall'alludere a un eventuale matrimonio della pupilla: il silenzio di Hodierna già tanto ansiosa di nozze per la figlia, le faceva sospettare una estrema penuria nelle casse del piccolo Stato. Senza denaro, senza terre con cui dotarla come si poteva maritare una ragazza che per nobiltà di sangue, bellezza, cultura non poteva convenire che a un principe di grande spicco? Così ragionando, a mente fredda, la badessa suppose che la sua ambiziosa sorella preferisse una figlia monaca a una figlia mal collocata o, peggio, destinata alle tristezze dello zitellaggio laico. Di conseguenza, quella tale speranza di trattenere per sempre a Betania la nipote non solo era rinata ma frondeggiava, torturata però da scrupoli che le suggerivano di sottoporre la giovinetta alle tentazioni della vanità. Vesti sontuose le furono dotate, e gioielli e profumi. Questa parte di inquisitore diabolico eccitava la badessa che, ora dopo ora, nelle più stimolanti circostanze, spiava le reazioni di Melisenda, giurando che questa volta l'esca era troppo allettante perché una fanciulla potesse resisterle. Rivestita di sete di ori e di gemme, essa avrebbe inevitabilmente desiderato quel che le era dovuto, uno sposo brillante, una corte gaia e fastosa. Insidie vane: la fanciulla guardò curiosamente i drappi e le gemme, li ammirò, ma neppure un istante fece l'atto di adattarli alla sua persona. Indossava, come le compagne, una lunga tunica di lana bianca, appena attillata alla vita: a due mani ne carezzò il tessuto e disse: ecco l'abito che preferisco, il più elegante del mondo. Queste parole, di per sé così eloquenti, furono accompagnate da un gesto non soltanto inatteso ma addirittura inconcepibile fra quelle pareti austere: la ragazza infatti, fece un passo avanti e abbracciò teneramente la zia: che, sbalordita per l'audacia non si accorse neppure di ricambiarla, tanto era gioiosamente indignata. Poi, a fatica ricomponendosi, Voi avete la febbre, sentenziò aggrottando la fronte, e la febbre vi fa trascendere. Andate, a letto, la speziale vi porterà una tisana. Il che non le impedì, chiusa in cella, di piangere di felicità.

Le feste pasquali si celebrarono quell'anno con eccezionale concorso di pellegrini, talché le piazze e le vie di Gerusalemme ne erano ricolme: le carovane giunte in gran numero dall'Oriente dovettero accamparsi a Gerico e lì svolgere i loro traffici. Smaniose di ammirare tanti tesori di paesi lontani e di assistere alle prodezze di mimi e giocolieri, le educande chiesero e ottennero di visitare, ben protette da suore e monaci, la fiera: erano così eccitate che Melisenda, nonostante la sua naturale inerzia, non seppe rifiutarsi di accompagnarle. Due giorni durò la loro assenza, al rientro le suore rimaste in convento le informarono che la badessa era incomodata e non usciva dal suo piccolo oratorio. Quando, alla fine, essa ricomparve a nessuna sfuggì l'alterazione dei suoi tratti, all'improvviso invecchiati, spogli del solito autoritario vigore. Pareva persino diminuita di statura, quasi rimpiccolita e più di tutte se ne doleva Melisenda credendola in pericolo di morte. Dopo un lieve cenno di saluto alle educande e l'esortazione a pregare facendo penitenza per la dissipazione della festa goduta, Joveta alzò la mano verso la nipote, una mano che tremava. Dopo la preghiera, disse, vi aspetto nella mia cella; e la sua voce era flebile, umiliata.

Dio ha chiamato a sé l'imperatrice Irene, queste le prime parole che essa pronunziò fissando Melisenda con gli occhi gonfi di chi ha lungamente pianto: poi, come non avesse la forza di proseguire, fece una pausa e l'ascoltatrice indifferente alla notizia ma oppressa da un arcano sbigottimento indietreggiava lottando con l'istinto di fuggire. E l'ha chiamata, riprese in tono più fermo Joveta, perché sul trono di Bisanzio sieda la più degna principessa d'Oltremare, Melisenda di Tripoli. Adesso la voce era solenne, dura, orgogliosa mentre fitte lacrime solcavano quelle guance avvizzite. L'imperatore Manuele ha chiesto la vostra mano, preparatevi a partire al più presto. Nel suo arretrare, la fanciulla sfiorava ormai col dorso la porta della cella: bruscamente fu spinta fuori e l'uscio si richiuse.

Ci si può opporre a un matrimonio d'amore, di diseguale condizione o di scarsa convenienza: ma non alla volontà dell'imperatore dei romani, simbolo della potenza divina. Contrastarla sarebbe un sacrilegio che né un sovrano, né un vescovo, né il papa — e figuriamoci una povera badessa mitrata — possono compiere. Nella sua agitazione Joveta non trova che un conforto; avere allevato un'imperatrice è un vanto che basta a illuminare un'intera vita e guai a chi, indulgendo ai moti del cuore, se ne rattristasse. Al pensiero di essersi illusa che una creatura così eletta potesse appartenerle, inorridisce: Dio l'ha punita inalzando alla luce del trono imperiale colei che essa pretendeva nascondere fra le mura di un chiostro. Genuflessa, la fronte a terra, prega per ottenere non la rassegnazione, ma uno smisurato orgoglio, l'unica medicina per un dolore come il suo. La visitano, infatti, immagini più che di fasto, di una solennità sacrale, la lingua con cui le enumera e definisce è la greca: ecco perché, riflette, si è tanto accanita ad apprenderla e a farla imparare a Melisenda: tutto era scritto, decreto del Signore.

Melisenda, intanto, dorme: il sonno è sempre stato la sua difesa contro la paura, il turbamenti, ogni genere di male. Appena distesa gli occhi le si chiudono, la mente si spenge. Non sogna, vola via in un mondo senza ricordi e al risveglio tutto è semplice. Così, seduta dinanzi al telaio, la trova al mattino la insonne badessa che vorrebbe, ma non osa, rammentarle il sublime destino che l'aspetta. Per un istante la mano che trapunge la tela s'immobilizza mentre le pupille violette paiono seguire nel vuoto un oggetto che sfugge. Infine, ripreso l'ago, chinata la testa, la fanciulla continua il suo ricamo. È chiaro, non vuol parlare e neppure Joveta lo vuole, bloccata da un rispetto senza fin che, in un attimo ha dissipato le angosce notturne e persino la stanchezza delle membra. Per lei Melisenda è già incoronata.

Per tutto il tempo che essa rimase a Betania, una settimana giusta, né lei né Joveta fecero più parola del matrimonio bizantino: astratta e pensosa la prima, impassibile la seconda, almeno all'aspetto. All'orgoglio con cui essa si sosteneva, si univa adesso la persuasione che la magnifica sorte della nipote riscattasse il proprio antico avvilimento di nubile che le sorelle, dai loro troni, avevano compianto ipocritamente. Cos'erano quei troni di fronte all'aureo soglio che Manuele offriva a Melisenda? Ma ecco, i tempi precipitano, i legati di Tripoli sono a Gerusalemme, una galea dalle vele purpuree è all'ancora a Jaffa in attesa della fidanzata. Nonostante il proposito di un distacco netto e rapido, la badessa annunzia che condurrà lei sua nipote sino al mare, l'ordine di Sant'Anna vi possiede una casa; lì, lontano da occhi indiscreti si scambieranno gli addii.

Così avvenne, sicché i curiosi non videro né lacrime né abbracci: sulla soglia del piccolo convento zia e nipote apparvero tenendosi per mano e subito si staccarono, Melisenda, fra i nuovi cortigiani dirigendosi alla riva, Joveta ferma nella sua dignità, finché il corteo non imboccò il ponte che univa la nave alla terraferma. Allora soltanto la porta si richiuse alle spalle della badessa. Poiché il conventino era provvisto di un'alta torre, qualcuno dagli occhi molto acuti asserì di scorgere lassù, appena emergente dai merli, una tunica bianca e un velo agitato dal vento: una notizia subito dispersa. Altro avevano da raccontare i mercanti e i marinai raccolti in folla a godere lo spettacolo dell'imbarco di una principessa che sposerà un imperatore. Sua madre, dicono, è carica di debiti, eppure le ha preparato un corredo tutto ricami e seta trapunta d'oro; ci hanno lavorato migliaia di schiave. Non si contano i mantelli di pellicce rare piovute dal settentrione, per i suoi gioielli l'India è stata saccheggiata e il conte Raimondo ha razziato tutta la costa e fin rubato i tesori delle chiese per allestire la flotta che scorterà la sorella a Bisanzio. A Tripoli si lavora per queste nozze giorno e notte e nessuno è pagato per la sua mercede. La corte è già colma di doni di principi, cristiani e mussulmani. Le carovane e le navi ne portano di nuovi ogni giorno.

Come monaca, anche se badessa, Joveta non possedeva denaro né oggetti preziosi: il suo dono a Melisenda fu una schiavetta turcomanna, da lei convertita, di estrema abilità e intelligenza. Allevata insieme alle educande di Betania ha superato tutte negli studi e negli esercizi del corpo, queste sue doti le hanno risparmiato le mansioni servili a cui era destinata. Ma quel che in lei prevale è l'acutezza del giudizio su fatti e persone, il potere quasi magico di leggere nei volti le intenzioni nascoste, gli intrighi più coperti. « Avrete in lei un fedele silenziario, un ambasciatore, una difesa: Azar sa usare la penna all'occorrenza, il pugnale, il veleno. Sarà lei a darmi ogni settimana vostre notizie e ad avvisarmi se un pericolo vi minaccia. Lei saprà informarvi della mia morte con parole che addolciranno il vostro dolore ». Così aveva scritto Joveta e Azar, dopo aver letto il messaggio alla nuova padrona, si era affrettata a distruggerlo.

Chi aveva affermato di vedere sulla torre una bianca figura e un velo svolazzante, non si era sbagliato, finché la galea non ruppe gli ormeggi e, via via si fu allontanata verso l'orizzonte, la badessa non ne staccò lo sguardo e così intensamente da illudersi di riconoscere, fra le dame d'onore imbarcate, la tunica di Melisenda che aveva rifiutato di deporre l'abito conventuale finché non fosse arrivata a Tripoli. Soltanto quando gli occhi, bruciati dal sole occiduo, non distinsero più che un mare di fuoco, si accorse di avere emesso un grido soffocato: Addio, figlia più che mia, dolcezza. Il velo s'inzuppava di lacrime, le mani le tremavano così forte che ne ebbe vergogna quasi non fosse sola e qualcuno spiasse la sua debolezza. D'istinto si asciugò in fretta la faccia e sollevò la fronte.

Non era sola, infatti, sulla scala che portava alla torre una bambinetta si era arrampicata e fissava su di lei gli occhi scuri, dalle folte ciglia di insetto. Sulle prime fu sicura di non conoscerla, solo percepiva rabbrividendo l'intenzione di quello sguardo immobile che malignamente la succhiava. Non si è monache senza superstiziose paure: Joveta credette a un'apparizione diabolica, preannuncio del castigo meritato dal suo eccessivo amore per Melisenda. Ma non tentò di sfuggirla, anzi si mosse per affrontarla subito e in quell'atto le tornò la memoria, la bruna bambina altri non era che Sibilla la figlia del defunto Amalrico e di Agnese di Courtenay,[10] sua moglie ripudiata e donna notoriamente lasciva: dunque sua pronipote e sorella del piccolo re lebbroso, il ragazzo più gentile del mondo. Ma come, unica fra le educande, Sibilla si trovava a Jaffa, chi ce l'aveva portata e perché?

Sebbene il caso fosse riprovevole, la badessa non alzò la voce, non intimò all'impertinente di scendere. Era stanca

---

[10]Amalrico, il figlio di re Folco di Gerusalemme, fu conte di Jaffa e Ascalon prima di succedere il fratello maggiore Baldovino III al trono nel 1163. Fu costretto ad annullare il suo matrimonio con Agnese di Courtenay perche era la sua cugina di terzo grado. Purtroppo Agnese riuscì a stabilire i diritti di legittimità e di eredità per suo figlio Baldovino e un'altra figlia.

di allevare bambine reali, destinate a innesti infelici e a moltiplicare inimicizie fra le parentele di Oltremare. Inoltre la discutibile innocenza di questa femminuccia, forse incaricata da sua madre di sostituirsi a Melisenda di Tripoli, la disgustava. È triste provare ripugnanza per un bambino, più triste ancora dissimulare, fingere di essergli amico. In silenzio, Joveta prende per mano la ragazzina e con lei scende la ripida scala: la tentazione di spingerla giù in fondo alla torre non dura che un attimo: ma c'è stata, ben chiara, in ogni particolare.

Non tardarono a Sant'Anna, i messaggi di Azar che tripudiava descrivendo gli addobbi, le bandiere, le giostre, i tornei in onore di Melisenda, finalmente ornata di vesti e gioielli degni della sua bellezza. Fra i doni più graditi, aggiungeva maliziosamente la piccola turcomanna, essa prediligeva un dischetto d'avorio e smalto, ritratto fedele, a quanto dicono, dell'imperatore Manuele. A corte se ne discute, giacché non molti l'hanno visto di persona e sono in grado di giudicare. Un bell'uomo di certo: viso pallido, occhi lunghi e stretti, naso ricurvo, capelli e barba di un nero corvino. Si mormora che la sua statura sia tutt'altro che imponente, Manuele è piccolo come tutti i Comneni suoi avi. Ma che importa? A Melisenda piace, il dischetto riccamente incorniciato, è appeso accanto al suo letto. Se innamorarsi di un ritratto è possibile, ebbene la principessa è innamorata del suo sposo.

Con questa affettuosa risatella si chiude, e un mese è passato, la corrispondenza di Azar: in Betania la badessa si angoscia fra dubbi, ipotesi, presentimenti. Per nulla al mondo si abbasserebbe a chiedere notizie alla corte del giovane re dove Agnese domina, sicché finisce per abbandonarsi alla speranza contentandosi di ragionamenti solitari: forse il viaggio della sposa è stato ritardato dal maltempo e Azar, puntigliosa, ha creduto inutile scrivere prima che la sua signora s'imbarcasse; forse qualche indiscreto le ha impedito di consegnare il solito messaggio a persona sicura. Incidenti, contrattempi plausibili, ma Joveta sente che c'è di peggio, che la sua immaginazione è impari agli avvenimenti e non sa imboccare la via della verità, quella che magari a quest'ora i carovanieri e i marinai della costa stanno raccontando, e a lei sola è negata.

Per confortarsi prende a rileggere l'ultima missiva di Azar, così frivola, ahimè, così sbadata. Maliziosamente sorpresa per il mutamento di Melisenda, la schiavetta ne riferiva le fasi: immemore del raccoglimento conventuale, degli innocenti piaceri di Betania, la futura imperatrice si dissipava nelle mondanità più vane, danzando, cantando storie d'amore, confidandosi con le più screditate damigelle di Tripoli: tanto presa di Manuele da mandarne a memoria la genealogia fin dai tempi che il grande Alessio Comneno non era ancora asceso al trono. Nei suoi discorsi dominava la certezza di essere appassionatamente amata e destinata a partorire un giorno nella gran sala purpurea il principe che Manuele avrebbe proclamato suo erede. Hodierna, d'altronde, secondava e plaudiva la metamorfosi della monachella: da bruco a farfalla, diceva. Per un attimo l'amarezza che la badessa aveva provato constatando la sua segreta sconfitta si scioglieva come una nuvola: immemore, lontana colla mente e col cuore, la soave Melisenda! Ma almeno viveva felice e questo le doveva bastare.

Credette di svenire invece quando, rotti i suggelli, lesse la lettera tanto attesa: Azar era ambigua, reticente, misurava le parole, evitava la chiarezza, si perdeva in notiziole superficiali che celevano il fondo delle cose. La data delle nozze non ancora stabilita, Raimondo furioso, il suo fedele Ottone di Risberg in viaggio per Bisanzio a chiarire le ragioni dell'indugio. In sostanza nulla di grave: eppure Melisenda è malinconica, per ore siede silenziosa, insensibile agli allettamenti della musica, alla conversazione, ai doni che tuttora arrivano. I mires che l'hanno visitata non le hanno scoperto alcun male, ma temono che delicata com'è, l'imminenza del matrimonio la turbi. Intanto le feste continuano, peccato che il tempo sia guasto, piove da una settimana, una benedizione per i contadini e anche per i signori che hanno feudi a cultura. Pesche e susine sono profumatissime, ma provocano disturbi talvolta pericolosi. Gervasio Parcy, un robusto capitano degli arceri, ne è morto.

Un tumulto di piazza (genovesi e veneziani venuti a contesa per certi privilegi da conquistare) fu l'occasione che diffuse a Sant'Anna la notizia che tutta Gerusalemme conosceva: Bisanzio è in festa per ricevere la giovane bellissima sposa di Manuele, partita non da Tripoli, ma da San Simone. E non si chiama Melisenda, esse è Maria di Antiochia, figlia di Costanza, nipote di Alice, ancora vincente, attraverso una fanciulla del suo sangue, nella gara fra gli stati di Oltremare. Joveta, indignata, tratta di pazzo l'informatore e considera la notizia una favola maligna. Non può essere, l'imperatore non ha che una parola egli non può disdirsi, accusarlo di tradimento è un delitto. Le monache, allibite, la sentono gridare forsennatamente, finché un greve silenzio succede alle urla. Ebbene, sì, Manuele ha rotto il trattato all'ultimo momento e la ragione c'è: gli ambasciatori, dopo aver riferito sulle mirabili doti della principessa, non hanno taciuto certe voci sulla sua nascita, frutto, secondo taluni, di una tresca adultera di Hodierna. E come potrebbe un così eccelso sovrano, correre il rischio di accogliere nel suo letto una bastarda?

Colpita al cuore, la badessa giace sul suo paglericcio, occhi sbarrati, volto esangue: con un gesto stanco ha allontanato le consorelle cui attraverso la porta chiusa giungono adesso i suoi deliri: che deliri non sono ma rigurgiti di antichi dolori taciuti, ingoiati in solitudine. Essa piange per quel che nessuno ha mai indovinato, le sue umiliazioni di principessa cadetta, muta spettatrice di passioni colpevoli, crocifissa nel suo amore per l'amante della regina. Forse, avida d'uomini come le sue sorelle, Hodierna ha davvero commesso l'adulterio di cui Melisenda è vittima e chissà dove il suo capriccio la trascinò. Toccherebbe a lei, adesso, sfatar la calunnia liberando la figlia dalla supposta ignominia di esser seme di un soldataccio o di uno schiavo. Ma ad altro pensano il conte e la contessa di Tripoli: lividi per lo scatto subito, si arrovellano per ricuperare il denaro del corredo e delle galee e pretendono, come mercanti falliti, che Manuele li risarcisca. Intanto frugano tra le dinastie di occidente alla ricerca di uno sposo che sostituisca l'imperatore.

È il disastro: il destino di Oltremare è segnato, comincia la resa dei conti di tanti omicidi, crudeltà, lussurie: la lebbra sta consumando le carni adolescenti dell'ultimo Baldovino: lui morto Gerusalemme cadrà in mano di Agnese che già pensa a uno sposo per la piccola Sibilla, il futuro re da usare come strumento di dominio. Crescendo, la ragazzina ha acquistato una torbida bellezza che molto si addice al ruolo che sua madre le affiderà. Per punto d'onore Joveta sovrintende alla sua educazione, ma un muro di gelo la divide da lei. Non sia mai, essa pensa inorridendo, che nelle memorie di Sant'Anna, redatte mese dopo mese dall'archivista del convento, il suo nome sia legato al nome di questa ragazza malfida. Ma in fondo nulla le importa quando la mente corre al capezzale di Melisenda, la cui malattia si è finalmente dichiarata e i mires di Tripoli le danno poche settimane di vita. Non soffre, non si lamenta ma non può reggersi in piedi e rifiuta ogni sorta di cibo. Data la dolcezza del clima riposa all'aperto, su un lettucio da campo, davanti al mare, gli occhi fissi sulle vele che sfrecciano e, di notte, sui lumicini delle zattere a cui le stelle fanno eco, lassù. È sempre bellissima, scrive Azar, ma come soffiata nel vetro. Sia fatta la volontà del Signore.

Una volontà misteriosa e contraddittoria se i mesi e gli anni passano e Melisenda continua a vivere, anzi ha ricominciato a nutrirsi e a restaurarsi con lunghi sonni profondi. Occupa le giornate divertendosi di giochi puerili molto quieti: si direbbe che col progredire dell'età — vent'anni compiuti — retroceda verso l'infanzia, un'infanzia sommessa. Ha perduto i colori: grigi gli stupendi occhi viola, le guance a fossette graffiate da due virgole sottilissime, opachi i capelli. Nessun segno di decadenza è trascurato nella descrizione di Azar che forse per essersi maritata a uno scudiero di Raimondo ha perduto, se non l'intelligenza, il garbo, la gentilezza d'animo. Ora essa parla della sua signora come di una vecchietta svanita che bisogna compatire: quasi mai l'imperatore l'avesse chiesta in moglie e la sua drammatica sconfitta appartenesse a una problematica leggenda.

Anche Joveta, impaziente di morire, indugia nella vecchiaia precoce, cucendo laboriosamente il mattino alla sera, la notte all'alba. Mentre aspetta la sua ora vive contentandosi di briciole stemperate nell'uniformità conventuale che ha finito per amare: la disputa di due suore litigiose, le risa delle educande più insolenti, la visita di qualche illustre pellegrina, sua parente alla lontana. La religione non le offre conforti da quando non ha più miracoli da chiedere e da credere, appassionatamente, di ottenere. Assidua, tuttavia, alle funzioni, spesso il mento le cade sul petto e il sonno che la notte la sfugge, l'appallottola in un gomitolo di bianche lane da cui vapora un respiro pesante. Da tali segni di senilità le madri più ambiziose deducono che sebbene non abbia passato di molto i sessant'anni, la badessa non potrà vivere a lungo: e chi le succederà? Madre Eva, la vicesuperiora, di poco più giovane, abbassa gli occhi modestamente: la protegge Agnese di Courtenay, che non promette invano.

Ma sembra che non sia così facile a Sant'Anna, cambiare di badessa: ogni tanto Joveta si risveglia dal suo torpore, squittiscono le sue battute ironiche, guizza il suo scetticismo verso tutti e tutto. Indovina l'impazienza di Eva e la sottolinea scherzando freddamente. Cosa speri, sogghigna, da una carica di badessa? Agnese ti tratterà come una vecchia ciabatta e se le negherai obbedienza non le mancheranno i mezzi per spedirti in esilio o all'altro mondo. Chiude gli occhi, ma le sue ciglia palpitano di malizia. E, a proposito, riprende, dove s'è ficcata quella basacetta di Sibilla? In mancanza di meglio quella è capace di infilarsi nel letto dell'ortolano. Madre Sara, sospira subito dopo, vedete voi di farle entrare in testa un po' di latino, magari quello di papa Gregorio che lo intendono anche i villani. È una principessa anche lei, dopo tutto e con la sua ignoranza potrebbe compromettere la fama di Betania. La miglior cosa sarebbe, pensa, ma non dice, rimandarla a corte, ma ha troppo rispetto per l'agonia del povero Baldovino, già insidiato dal partito di Agnese per turbarlo con la presenza di una sorella irrequieta ed egoista. Del resto, quel che ha da succedere succederà, il tempo è gravido d'imprevisti.

Fra gli imprevisti Joveta sogna un evento favoloso: Melisenda di Tripoli, risanata di corpo e di mente, può aspirare a un trono suo, legittimamente acquisito. Il prezzo è la morte di Raimondo e quella Hodierna, tutt'altro che improbabili con tutti i nemici che hanno. Unica erede, Melisenda governerà con la saggezza e l'intelligenza che la distinguevano a Betania. La consiglierà, del resto, la stessa Joveta che lascerà il suo convento e la sua mitra per trasferirsi a Tripoli accanto alla nipote. Essa rimugina tutto un programma di riforme da suggerire e sperimentare: nuove alleanze da stringere non già con l'occidente, ma con principi di popolazioni orientali bellicose, impazienti di affacciarsi al mare; favorire le industrie indigene e i commerci, creare una flotta potente, dare esempio di una giustizia immune da pregiudizi, da privilegi, praticare più la clemenza che la severità; infine proibire le scorrerie, i saccheggi di villaggi e carovane. Ma soprattutto operare per una pacifica intesa delle religioni. A questo fine Joveta conta di valersi di una specie di senato femminile, convinta che le donne tendano più alla concretezza della vita che all'astrazione omicida delle idee. Ad esse, inoltre, sarà affidata la sorveglianza della salute pubblica, tanto negletta dai crociati fin dal loro primo arrivo in Palestina.

All'alba, questi sogni a occhi aperti cedono a un assopimento che li divora, mentre si ricompongono i duri contorni della realtà: Baldovino muore, e lassù, in Siria, Melisenda continua il suo ruolo di eterna bambina, senza volontà né desideri. Queste esistenze scomparse o languenti, questo lungo malinconico tramonto di giovani astri sono frutto della maledizione che Dio ha pronunziato contro chi si è servito della Croce per soddisfare la brama di ricchezze e di potenza: tanto dire tutti i baroni di Oltremare, poveri a casa loro e, all'improvviso, potenti capi di famiglie corrotte. Adesso nella sua testa indebolita i fili delle parentele si annodano come in una matassa inestricabile, nomi vecchi e nomi nuovi saltellano quasi cavallette sulla terra arsa. Chi è, per esempio, questo Guido di Lusignano che Sibilla vuole sposare, tradendo la fede data a un Ibelin? Il tempo scorre come un fiume attraverso il cervello della badessa, gli anni vi si accavallano. Dunque Sibilla non è più in Betania: quando ne è uscita?

Dio è lontano, i suoi segni sono avvolti nella nebbia del futuro, quando la nebbia si scioglie ci accorgiamo che essi sono già padroni dell'orizzonte. Alternando oscure profezie ad assenze della memoria la ormai decrepita badessa ha ancora momenti di fervore durante i quali sempre più spesso pronunzia il nome di Saladino.[11] Lo chiamo il trionfatore, il clemente, il saggio. Non sono così vecchia, dice, da non poter vederlo signore di Gerusalemme. Le suore si tappano le orecchie ma le più anziane borbottano che non c'è da stupirsi, Joveta è sempre stata più mussulmana che cristiana, l'hanno allevata le donne di Timurtash.

---

[11]Sultano d'Egitto e di Siria. Conquise Gerusalemme nel 1187.

« Da allora; da allora è cambiato! » Uguali le parole, uguale l'accento con cui Marie Gabrielle confida la sua pena di madre tradita. È una donna ancor giovane, succhiata dall'angoscia, tutta capelli e occhi e sempre si guarda intorno con sospetto. Il suo unico figlio le ha teso la fronte per il bacio mattutino, una fronte bombata, caparbia, che più di offrirsi si sottrae, lei non riesce che a sfiorarne i capelli. « Ha visto, Léonie? Vada, vada e faccia attenzione... ».

Jean ha adesso tredici anni e un carattere chiuso, difficilissimo. E si capisce. Mai esce solo, per lui non esistono le scuole pubbliche, qualcuno lo ha decretato, evidentemente suo padre, grande industriale ricchissimo, inutile insistere. Ma nessuno si sogna di infrangere questa regola, tanto meno il ragazzo, avvezzo da anni a ricevere giornalmente quando due, quando tre professori. Lavora abbastanza bene, senza sforzi, ma potrebbe, se volesse, fare di più. Lui non vuole, questo è chiaro, il suo fine è dimostrare che gli studi, sebbene addolciti, pastorizzati da docenti di alto livello, non lo interessano affatto. Soltanto al principio di giugno, quando ogni anno deve presentarsi agli esami di privatista, un briciolo di animazione illumina i suoi occhi celesti. È una specie di rito, ma, come ogni cerimonia rigidamente predisposta, suscettibile d'imprevisti. Così, almeno, spera il ragazzo: senonché basta l'aspetto della macchina nera e acciaio, dello chauffeur bardato (dalla visiera lucida ai guanti massicci) a togliergli puntualmente ogni illusione. Velocissima la macchina percorre un tragitto senza semafori, volta l'angolo del licée e si ferma, precisissima, davanti a un usciòlo secondario: sul marciapiede si gingillano con vari arnesi due operai in tuta fiammante che si raddrizzano fissando lo sportello da cui Jean discende. Due passi, due rampe di scala a chiocciola, e si trova nella solita aula, davanti al tavolo dell'esame. Le sue riposte sono corrette, non soffre di timidezza o di complessi, la sua memoria è lucida: ottiene voti sufficienti, nulla di più. Dopo un'ora scende, ripassa la porticina. Alla sua destra, a una ventina di metri di distanza si apre un gran portone dinanzi a cui vociano e si agitano gruppi di studenti, ma lui non si volta, non li guarda: come se non esistessero. Rientrato in casa, riprende la lettura — un libro qualunque — interrotta. Oggi, i professori non verranno, l'anno è finito, domani si parte per i Vosgi. « Ebbene, come è andata? » chiede con giovialità fittizia il padre quando lo incontra a colazione. « Ma... bene, credo » risponde Jean, pensando: « Se sapesse quanto me ne importa! »; intanto il padre gli ha battuto sulla spalla liquidando in fretta la situazione. Si siedono a tavola, ma si rialzano di scatto quando entra in sala la madre, la moglie. Un saluto rapido al marito, un'occhiata ansiosa al figlio. « Sei stanco, caro? Hai appetito? » Gli prende la mano per il polso, come per tastarglielo, lo bacia in fronte strisciandovi le labbra e saggiandone la temperatura. Si siede, spiega il tovagliolo. Il marito dice: « Fagli i rallegramenti, l'esame è andato bene ». « Ah, sì? » Marie Gabrielle si serve di antipasti, avvertendo il cameriere: « Non del pâté per M. Jean, prego, è troppo indigesto ».

Per i Vosgi partono soltanto Jean e sua madre. Più M.lle Léonie, che ha sostituito la nurse Janine di quando era piccolo: più il vecchio Jérémie, colle fedine. Non portano bagagli, tutto quel che occorre, compresi i domestici, li attende in campagna. Lassù non si starebbe male, anche se il castello restaurato pieno di statue, di arazzi e di mobili Rinascimento è tutt'altro che ameno. Il parco è vasto, c'è il tennis, un lago, una scuderia di cavalli da sella, un canile selezionato. Ma come goderne sotto gli occhi allarmati, imploranti, di una donna che soffre di nervi? La custodia è più stretta, più ossessiva che a Parigi. Nei viali, mai che si possa evitare la presenza di giardinieri e guardiacaccia che appena Jean si muove gli si mettono, a coppia, alle calcagna: alle sue occasionali domande rispondono brevi e confusi. Un paio di ragazzi, figli di proprietari delle ville vicine, sarebbero compagni gradevoli, ma ormai Jean sa per esperienza che loro si seccano: alla prima proposta di uscire dal parco per una gita, per una corsa in città, un week-end a venti miglia, compare la mutria di Jérémie ad opporre che non è possibile, si divertano qui i signorini.

Ma quei ragazzi ricchi non sanno che farsene del tennis, del bagno sorvegliato e della trottata entro la cinta del parco, subito i loro occhi si distolgono e si volgono in direzione del cancello, è chiaro che fra cinque minuti si congederanno con una scusa. Quanto a Jean, lui non protesta, non accetta né rifiut a i diversivi, non tenta di trattenere i compagni. Appare distratto, indifferente. Stringe loro la mano un po' all'antica, scuotendola dal basso in alto e volta i passi verso casa, giocherellando con quel che si trova fra le dita, un ramoscello, una palla, un frustino, flebili richiami a svaghi abortiti. Inevitabilmente, prima di varcarne la soglia incontrerà M.lle Léonie, ferma dinanzi alla scalinata. « Rientri così presto, Jean? È un tempo delizioso... ». Spesso Jean non le risponde, a volte fa un gesto vago e accelera il passo. Traversa l'atrio sonoro dalle panoplie rugginose, sale lo scalone di quercia, volta per la scaletta di servizio, la percorre di volo quasi incalzato da un pericolo, quello, in effetti, di trovarsi di fronte il viso consunto di Marie Gabrielle, di sentir la sua voce scoraggiata: « Caro, sei sudato? Perché corri? Chi c'era in giardino? Rimani in camera? » Insopportabile.

Il volto di sua madre se lo ricorda sempre così, chiuso da un accento circonflesso che dalla radice del naso le spiove sugli occhi. Eppure se spinge e sforza il suo sguardo interno, se solleva la barrieta opaca, dietro cui — sogni o ricordi — vivono di luce chiara immagini non identificabili, riesce ad intravedere un viso ridente dalle guance rosate vicinissimo al suo, mentre voci gioiose intorno chiamano « Marie Gabrielle! » Ricercare in questo aspetto oscuramente commovente i tratti dell'attuale Marie Gabrielle è una fatica che Jean respinge, d'istinto. Lo disgusta l'idea che chi è vecchio sia stato giovane e chi è giovane possa invecchiare: per lui sua madre è vecchia, come si è biondi o castani, dalla nascita. Inoltre le donne gli danno uno strano disagio, misto di noia e di diffidenza.

Non è mai stato curioso, questo ragazzo; non ha mai chiesto agli adulti la ragione delle cose, bastandogli quella che raggiunge da solo, in lente e frammentarie deduzioni. Del resto gli adulti non gli ispirano fiducia: un po' di più crederebbe ai coetanei, se gli fosse dato di starci insieme a lungo, in modo da capire cosa pensano, senza far domande. Che questa possibilità non sia alla sua portata è un fatto che non discute, di cui non si duole: la sua mancanza di curiosità si accompagna ad una grande pazienza, una qualità che nessuno gli ha imposto o consigliato. L'ha scelta da sé, alteramente, e l'ha acquistata con un lungo segreto esercizio. Ma a che cosa gli serve e gli servirà non pensa, anche perché non aspetta nulla, non fantastica sul suo futuro, anzi non ne ha voglia. Vagamente indovina che, finiti gli studi, suo padre gli offrirà di « lavorare in ditta », come fanno gli zii, i loro figli e nipoti. È tuttavia convinto che questo destino potrà benissimo evitarlo se proprio non gli piacerà. Ma qui sta il punto: cosa piacerà a Jean cui nulla piace?

Piano: gli piace questo: fermarsi davanti alla porta della sua camera e immobile, impassibile, raggiungere la sicurezza che nessuno lo abbia seguito e lo spii. Poi, lentamente girare la maniglia ed entrare richiudendosi senza rumore la porta alle spalle. Col paletto.

Un gesto che è una vittoria. Con esso Jean ha sconfitto ciò che più odia, la paura. Ma non la propria, che non è mai esistita. Quella degli altri, quella soprattutto, di sua madre che ne trabocca, che ne è invecchiata. Dipendono da lei tutti i segni di paura che costellano la sua vita limitata, circoscritta da un allarme sordo e costante: Jérémie, Léonie, il guardiacaccia, il giardiniere; e gli stessi cavalli, i cani, le automobili, il motoscafo del lago: pronti e inutili con l'ipocrita offerta: quando vuoi, come vuoi. Se Jean accettasse, tutta una catena di paure cigolerebbe, lui ne ha, preventivamente, una specie di mal di mare. In camera sua, invece, in campagna come in città, tutto si apre al suo arbitrio, la sua volontà è incontrollata.

« ... e non so proprio come impieghi il suo tempo. No, non legge molto, la più parte dei suoi libri non li tocca, non sono nemmeno tagliati. Sì, qualche volta suona. Ma non il piano, non ha voluto studiarlo. La chitarra, certe nenie strane. È il suo cuore che non funziona, non la sua testa, credetelo. Era così tenero da piccolo, così affettuoso.

Poi a un tratto, tac, qualcosa si è fermato in lui. È stato nel momento che me lo hanno riportato, dopo giorni e giorni di incubo, pensate! Era roseo e tranquillo: come l'ho stretto fra le braccia è scoppiato in singhiozzi. Credevo per la gioia di rivedermi. Ma da allora, non una parola, non un segno di affetto per me. Ogni mattina, ogni sera, la fronte da baciare e via. Vi rendete conto? C'è da impazzire... ».

Così geme, da anni, Marie Gabrielle e Jean lo sa, più volte, senza volerlo, l'ha udita, oppresso da un triste pudore che è pietà e insieme ribrezzo e lo rende incapace di un gesto, muto. Il dolore di sua madre lo raggiunge materialmente, come una sostanza vischiosa che riempia l'aria di casa, si attacchi ai vetri delle finestre e che solo la porta della sua stanza respinge. Qui non entrano i suoi singhiozzi soffocati, né la sua folle paura, come non penetrano i custodi sornioni, Léonie e Jérémie. Qui avvengono le scoperte di Jean, i suoi viaggi, le sue avventure. Di altro non ha bisogno che di queste quattro pareti. Vi potrebbe ricevere, se lo desiderasse, un cugino, un compagno: ma lui non ci tollera nessuno, neanche la cameriera che per mettere ordine e rifargli il letto deve approfittare delle sue brevi assenze. E anche questa indispensabile intromissione di un'estranea preferisce ignorarla. Quando torna dalla prescritta passeggiata mattutina ha l'illusione che l'ordine si sia fatto da sé magicamente: tante cose, nel supercomfort della sua famiglia, hanno l'apparenza di un atto di magia...

Disponibile, finalmente libero, si accinge ai pochi atti (e gli paion mille) che esprimono le sue vere scelte. Si avvicina alla libreria, ne trae un volume, lo sfoglia, ne legge qualche pagina; tenta le corde della chitarra, prova una nuova posizione delle dita; apre la cassetta dei pastrelli, sfila dal blocco un foglio da disegno. Ed eccolo impegnato nel solito soggetto: un mare tempestoso su cui naviga un grande tre alberi a vele spiegate, minutamente descritto in tutti i suoi accessori. Per caso uno di questi disegni capitò un giorno sott'occhio a suo padre che ne rimase impressionato. « Perbacco, un ingegnere navale in erba. È un'indicazione preziosa, amico mio ». Sotto la solita manata amichevole la spalla del ragazzo scivolò via mentre dalle palpebre socchiuse filtrava un focherello ironico, quasi una scintilla di riso. Il padre, c'era questo di buono, non si affliggeva affatto per i suoi modi evasivi, non li rilevava neppure. Dichiarava che i ragazzi vanno lasciati vivere. « Non fosse stato per mia moglie... » soggiungeva con un sospiro. Naturalmente quando il figliolo non era presente.

Nei vascelli disegnati con tanta esattezza e tanto amore era la chiave del segreto di Jean, un segreto ben guardato perché lui solo ne era partecipe, e tanto gelosamente lo custodiva da trattenersi dal richiedere l'unico oggetto che desiderasse: una di quelle bottiglie nel cui esiguo interno è entrato, non si sa come, un intero bastimento. Questo desiderio rimontava a qualche anno innanzi, precisamente al giorno che, tenuto per mano da M.lle Léonie, era passato dinanzi ad una vetrina dove, fra vecchi libri era esposto, appunto, un veliero in bottiglia. Di colpo lui si era fermato, tanto che la donna aveva quasi perduto l'equilibrio. E subito a domandargli: « Cosa guardi, cos'è che ti piace? » Come avvertito di un pericolo Jean si era ripreso e si era rimesso a camminare. « Niente », aveva detto.

Da allora, per controllare e insieme stimolare il senso dell'impressione ricevuta, Jean ricercò libri di viaggi, di avventure di mare, copiosamente illustrati. Non gli piacevano i transatlantici, le navi moderne, lo incantavano le vecchie incisioni di vascelli a vele spiegate, dalle intricate attrezzature. Li osservava avidamente e a lungo, poi chiudeva il libro e, a memoria, prendeva a disegnare: fogli e fogli si coprivano di fantasmi di velieri che via via si definivano sempre più precisi nelle loro linee, nei loro cordami tesi. E, all'improvviso, lasciava cadere la matita e chiudeva gli occhi. Dietro le palpebre serrate ecco aprirsi, finalmente raggiunta, una stanza (forse la cabina del capitano?) ovattata di tappeti, di bassi divani, di spessi tendaggi variopinti. Ancora uno sforzo, e compare uno scaffale sui cui ripiani non poggiano libri, ma bizzarri oggetti, pugnali nella loro guaina, statuette, soprattutto bottiglie con dentro navicelle di ogni forma. Jean sa che questi oggetti li ha toccati uno per uno, che sono lisci o ruvidi, pesanti o leggeri e glieli porge una mano bruna che scende dall'alto per lui. Intanto qualcuno canta, una voce bassa e molle, accompagnata dal vibrare sommesso di uno strumento a corda e basta voltarsi un pochino per scorgere una faccia scura che sorride con tutti i suoi denti bianchissimi.

Adesso, a tredici anni, Jean è persuaso che queste immagini recuperate non sono sogni, ma veri ricordi della sua primissima infanzia, gli unici che si stacchino, desiderabili, dal suo lontano passato pieno di sensazioni monotone, di figure ovvie, di giochi insulsi, di paesaggi verdi senza rilievo: un passato di noia. Dacché ha avuto coscienza di sé il suo istinto gli ha detto che deve lottare, passivamente, per conservarli e non lasciarli sommergere nel lago delle sue giornate senza difficoltà; mentre la madre e i familiari tendono a tutto potere a cancellarli dalla sua memoria.

C'è un ripostiglio segreto, nella sua stanza di città: dietro un armadio a muro Jean ha scoperto, fra legno e intonaco una fessura, uno spazio sottile, sufficiente tuttavia a contenere e nascondere dei fogli di carta ben ripiegati e compressi. È stata una scoperta preziosa perché altrimenti come avrebbe potuto nascondere certi ritagli di giornale che, negli ultimi tempi, è venuto raccogliendo? Il modo come ne è venuto a conoscenza e se n'è impadronito è di per sé un'avventura, una favola da cui la sua solitudine ha tratto nuovo nutrimento ed esaltazione estrema.

Il fatto era avvenuto d'estate, in campagna, di primo pomeriggio: quel giorno lui aveva resistito ostinatamente a Léonie che insisteva, come al solito, per ricondurlo a casa per la siesta. A quel tempo si era incapricciato del figlio del cuoco, un ragazzetto rubicondo e robusto che volentieri gli lasciavano frequentare. Alla famiglia del cuoco era stato concesso di abitare un padiglione del parco che a Jean pareva di gran lunga preferibile al castello, magari gli avessero permesso di dormirci. Stufo di giocare a tamburello col signorino, Victor gli aveva detto: « Vieni in casa, che ti mostro la radio costruita da mio fratello »: e Léonie aveva dovuto acconsentire, sedendosi al fresco accanto alla porta del padiglione. Dall'esame della radio i due ragazzi erano passati a trastullarsi con diversi aggeggi tratti da un armadio: e l'armadio era rimasto aperto. « Ti sei dimenticato questo pezzo » fece Jean togliendo dal ripiano dove era deposto un elemento del meccano che il compagno, ginocchioni per terra, s'ingegnava a montare: e in quell'istante vide sul vecchio giornale che foderava l'asse il proprio ritratto di quando era piccolo, lo stesso che sua madre teneva sullo scrittoio. Sotto c'era stampato: « Jean B., il bambino rapito ». Il suo nome.

« Scommetto che non ci riesci » articolò lentamente voltando le spalle al mobile. Si sentiva freddo, orgoglioso, un gigante, mentre la mano nascosta dietro la schiena incideva profondamente con l'unghia il foglio polveroso.

L'operazione gli riuscì a meraviglia, il brano inciso pareva tagliato con le forbici. Lo strinse in pugno; ma non troppo perché non si sciupasse ed ebbe la fermezza di rimanere ritto e impassibile per qualche minuto a guardare Victor che armeggiava inutilmente. « Te l'avevo detto che non ci riuscivi » concluse staccandosi dall'armadio senza neppure richiuderne i battenti; « Be', adesso sono stanco, vado a dormire, ciao ». Aveva infilato in tasca la pallottola di carta e si avviava alla porta.

Purtroppo, oltre la foto, ben pochi particolari forniva il ritaglio: ma a Jean bastò la certezza di essere stato rapito, di aver dunque passato del tempo (giorni, mesi?) lontano dai suoi in un luogo misterioso. Il frammento portava la data del giorno in cui il rapimento era avvenuto e per poco esperto che fosse, il ragazzo era sicuro che con quel riferimento avrebbe potuto procurarsi tutti i giornali che avevan parlato dell'episodio. Preparato, come al solito, ad aver pazienza, non si aspettava che il caso lo favorisse così presto, e fu il giorno che per un attaco più grave del consueto Marie Gabrielle aveva attratto su di sé l'attenzione di tutti i familiari. Lo studio del padre era rimasto aperto, aperta sul tavolo una cartella di documenti, e i documenti erano, appunto, ritagli di giornali. Senza chiedersi come mai essa fosse stata abbandonata a quel modo Jean leggeva a sobbalzi, gli occhi gli saltavan da una riga all'altra in esasperata affannosa attenzione. Rubò qualche ritaglio, communque conobbe per intero l'episodio drammatico che aveva segnato la sua prima infanzia: e d'un tratto seppe anche quel che nessuno sapeva, l'aspetto del luogo dove i rapitori l'avevan condotto e di chi gli era stato accanto: i protagonisti dei suoi sogni-ricordi che nebbiosamente o vivacemente a seconda delle ore, gli apparivano come esseri a lui congeniali, affini: i suoi veri amici.

Era stato in mano loro per venti giorni, a quanto raccontavano i giornali. Si eran sospettati i domestici, la nurse Janine, impiegati di suo padre, persino amici di casa; qualcuno aveva fornito presunti connotati del loro viso della loro statura. Si cercavano uomini biondi, dall'aspetto nordico, uomini piccoli e tarchiati, una donna bruna. Sciocchi, rideva Jean che a forza di interrogarsi, di forzare la su memoria era riuscito ad accostare al suonatore di chitarra altre due figure, due uomini alti e magri anche essi di pelle fosca, anch'essi sorridenti in gesti graziosi di offerta: una tazza di cioccolato, la vivanda che lui da piccolo preferiva, gran vassoi di paste. Cos'altro? Vedeva certi curiosi gingilli bianchi e neri con cui si era trastullato e riconosceva adesso come pezzi di scacchi. Ma soprattutto e nel modo più chiaro ricordava i vascelli in bottiglia: di averli toccati, maneggiati, forse sciupati. Come eran venuti fuori dal vetro? Certo qualcuno, al suo desiderio, ne aveva spezzato l'involucro. Insieme alla voce che cantava e al ronzare della chitarra, rammentava altri suoni, brevi sillabe pronunziate sommessamente con straordinaria dolcezza. I rapitori gli parlavano in una lingua ignota che lui, allora, aveva accolto come la conoscesse. E l'impressione definitiva era di aver trattato con coetanei, cioè di essere, lui, piccolissimo, adulto, maturo, una sensazione meravigliosa.

Apprese che i « banditi » (i giornali li chiamavano così) avevan chiesto per il suo riscatto una grossa somma di denaro che il padre aveva pagato senza batter ciglio. Ne era contento, trovava giusto che la loro rischiosa azione, preparata con tanta intelligenza, fosse stata premiata dal successo. Stimava suo padre per aver mantenuto lealmente l'impegno di non aiutare la polizia nella ricerca dei colpevoli. Disprezzava, invece, il nonno paterno che aveva passato ai giornali il numero di seri delle banconote versate. Istintivamente aveva sempre detestato quel vecchio che, la domenica, incontrava alla chiesa evangelica: giacca nera, pantoloni a righe, spalle enormi, e sempre in piedi col libro dei salmi aperto sulle grosse mani. Naturale che i rapitori avessero risposto minacciando un nuovo e definitivo ratto del bambino: ed ecco donde era scaturita la morbosa paura di Marie Gabrielle, l'incubo che aveva gravato sull'infanzia de Jean. Magari, mi avessero di nuovo rapito, si augurava il ragazzo, sarei a quest'ora uno di loro, chissà dove, nei loro paesi. E mia madre mi avrebbe dimenticato.

Una grande passione per gli atlanti e i mappamondi sostituì ora quella per i velieri e la chitarra: sulle carte geografiche delle regioni più remote la sua fantasia si sbrigliava. Erano stati bravi, i suoi amici, non si erano lasciati prendere e, ormai ricchi, avevano raggiunto luoghi inaccessibili dove vivevano come principi misteriosi, occupati in imprese temerarie. Non c'erano donne fra loro, a cosa servivano le donne se non a impicciare come aveva fatto Marie Gabrielle? Un giorno Jean li avrebbe cercati, raggiunti, portandogli tutto il denaro che potesse, e vivrebbe con loro, partecipe di una regola dura e forte che gli era venuta in mente leggendo la storia degli « Assassini ».

Ma nell'autunno dei suoi quattordici anni, la vita di Jean mutò radicalmente. « Sei abbastanza grande per frequentare le scuole pubbliche » gli annunziò il padre con insolita gravità, e questa volta la sua mano sulla spalla del ragazzo insisteva con una specie di nuovo calore. « Siamo due uomini soli, ormai » aggiunse con una smorfia amara « la mamma dovrà curarsi a lungo ». Marie Gabrielle, infatti, non era tornata dalla campagna che per entrare in clinica: Jean del resto ne era già informato: malattia mentale, dicevano. M.lle Léonie, passata governante di casa, non si curava più del ragazzo che si trovò libero di uscire solo, a suo piacere. Il primo giorno di scuola venne a prenderlo suo cugino Jacques che aveva tre anni più di lui, un giovanotto. Lo aveva praticato pochissimo e non gli era, come tutta la tribù dei parenti, per niente simpatico. Adesso si dava delle arie: « Be', era tempo che rientrassi nella normalità e tuo padre non doveva cedere come ha fatto alle ubbie morbose di tua madre. Dopo tutto se avesse reagito subito alle sue paure inconsulte, sarebbe stato meglio anche per lei ».

Scomparsa la macchina nera e acciaio, giubilato il vecchio Jérémie, ridotto il numero dei domestici, le giornate di Jean risultarono anziché piene di novità, vuote e disorientate. Va bene, era un uomo, ma a che cosa gli serviva adesso il suo lungo tirocinio di pazienza, come appagare il suo gusto ancora infantile per l'avventura? Nel suo cuore rimasto solitario il vento dell'improvvisa libertà disperdeva minaccioso i feticci dell'infanzia, quei sogni-ricordi che avevano arrestato la sua vita: ora non era più tanto sicuro della loro realtà né di voler rintracciare, un giorno, quelli che chiamava i suoi amici. Da prigioniero non si era mai confidato con nessuno, non ne aveva bisogno, ma adesso sentì che a forza di tacere, anche la propria identità si sarebbe smarrita. Fu così che una mattina, in un bar di studenti assordato dal juke-box, osò portare il cugino sui loro comuni ricordi infantili, quando giocavano insieme al Bois. Jacques, seduto di fronte a lui, lo ascoltava appena, guardava una ragazzetta e, col piede, seguiva il ritmo del disco; anche Jean, del resto, ostentava un tono beffardo, imparato da poco. « Proprio due bei cretini eravamo, ma tu più di me che a sei anni non sapesti neppur dire di che colore fossero quei tipi che mi portarono via. Va bene che era gente in gamba e infatti si è visto da come hanno saputo prendere il largo con tutto il malloppo. In fondo... », in fondo, voleva aggiungere, ne conservo la nostalgia. Jacques avrebbe riposto: « E che, te ne ricordi ora? »

Invece lui lo guardava fisso, così sorpreso che il lighter con cui stava accendendo la sigaretta quasi gli bruciava le dita. « Ma che stai contando » sbottò. « Io stetti zitto perché tuo padre me lo impose formalmente e il mio ci litigò persino. Poi la zia si fissò che ti avrebbero riacchiappato e lo zio non volle contraddirla, anche quando li ebbero messi dentro, due anni dopo. Vent'anni, si presero, erano gente della casbah. Che, non lo sapevi? »

Le ultime parole furono coperte da un gran fracasso: il cameriere, passando, era stato urtato da un cliente e il vassoio che reggeva era caduto in terra schizzando intorno cocci e caffè bollente. Col fazzoletto Jean si smacchiava i calzoni, poi alzò la testa: « Lo sapevo benissimo » disse « ma so anche che la polizia ha preso un granchio, i veri responsabili non li hanno mai rintracciati ». Le labbra gli tremavano, ma riuscì a dominarsi. « Mi passi una gauloise? » chiese.

LA SIGNORINA

Le paiono tanti, ventitré anni: un tramonto. Ma la gente non la pensa così e allora per dignità, per buona creanza, deve comportarsi come se ne avesse diciotto, ridere, dissimulando questo sentirsi terribilmente adulta. Già s'era allarmata quando, allo scoccare dei venti il suo nome — sino allora un infantile nome di battesimo — divenne, in casa e fuori, « la signorina ». Era la toga pretesta,[1] una investitura immutabile, a meno che... Dall'alternativa sottintesa, essa cercava scampo alzando le spalle, sapeva però di non potere evitare, almeno a giudizio degli altri, la candidatura a una promozione. E ne aveva gran fastidio.

Il suo alleato fu una passione difficile: voluta, accettata, astrattamente imperiosa. Non si ama per vincere, per conquistare la vita: la vita fu tutta una silenziosa sequenza di angosce, rotte — non dissipate — da scintille di effimera, turbata esaltazione. Avari, i miracoli: pure avvenivano, il passo dell'Amato che si avvicinava aveva dell'apparizione. Infatti, eccolo là, consente ad esistere. Per un'ora — o per qualche minuto — cammina con lei, scorrono parole, magari un po' disattente e tutte la

[1]Una toga bianca con orlo di porpora, prima indossata da un magistrato dall' Antica Roma, e poi da un ragazzo prima che indossasse la toga viriles à 15 anni e da una ragazza fino al matrimonio.

colgono in pieno petto, talvolta pugnali, ma non importa, il sangue ristagna. Lei, rigida per pudore, come un soldato che ha paura e finge di aver coraggio.

Non poteva durare e non durò. Cosa sono tre anni di batticuori, di desolate attese, di delusioni scontate? Un lampo. Il cimento più amaro, più difficile da sostenere, fu quando, convalescente — grandi occhi pesti, viso estenuato — sperò di apparirgli così delicatamente leggiadra da intenerirlo. Prima di uscire si era guardata allo specchio: una pastorella, con quella larga pamela fiorita di violette e quel vestitino verde acqua che la rendeva trasparente. Un fiasco. L'Adorabile era aggrondato, impaziente. È finita, si disse — e le lacrime a pungere senza traboccare; la voce — un violino, secondo i compagni all'università — ad arrancare divagando, a esorcizzare con inezie la catastrofe, quell'addio sempre presentito: non per oggi, sembra, lui ha fretta, il saluto è rapido ma non definitivo. Le labbra secche rifiutarono di aprirsi per il timido « a domani » : e già era sola, e la seta leggera della veste pesava come piombo, le era tornata la febbre.

Una lenta estate di assenza, qualche rara lettera, gli ultimi esami, la laurea. (« Ah già, dimenticavo, mi sono laureata ».) È di regola questo ostentato distacco dalle vicende accademiche. Lui si ferma per accendere una sigaretta, aspira: « Complimenti ». A che serve camminare ancora una volta insieme? Ah, ecco: « Dovresti farmi un piacere, mi hanno regalato un cucciolo maltese, l'ho promesso per Natale agli amici C. Me lo terresti per un paio di mesi? Magari ti ci diverti, è carino ».

Ha ritrovato in un cassetto una vecchia fotografia, formato cartolina: il documento di una quasi solenne infelicità, l'impresa araldica della sconfitta accettata. Ricorda: ore vuote in questo autunno terribilmente libero, uscire o rimanere in casa si valgono e così la solitudine o una casuale compagnia. Un'amica di passaggio, un parco pubblico, un fotografo dilettante (chi sarà mai stato?) quanto occorreva perché in una immagine si concretasse l'inevitabile. Non ascoltata, l'amica chiacchierava, il cucciolo tenuto al guinzaglio seguiva a passetti minuti la temporanea padrona: adorava ed era adorato. La penombra del bosco favoriva come in un dormiveglia tenuissime speranze: forse il patto non sarà osservato, privarla della bestiola sarebbe troppo crudele. Aveva detto: « me lo consegni a tuo comodo, la settimana di Natale ». Lei aveva puntato su una dimenticanza, i disgraziati si attaccano a tutto. Se me lo lascia, non fosse che per giocare con Toby c'incontreremo ancora. Sa di illudersi ma non osa negarsi questo minimo respiro.

Gli aveva cucito a modo di collare una gorgeretta[2] di seta scozzese, una specie di golilla spagnola; « un amore »,

[2] Dal francese « gorgerette ». Una specie di mantellina che copre il collo e scende sulle spalle.

la gente si fermava ad ammirarlo, a carezzarlo. Mai aveva supposto che quei complimenti fossero un pretesto per un approccio galante: lei era fuori gioco, lei non esisteva. La bloccò come una sorpresa l'invito del giovane fotografo a posare su quella panchina rustica (« sola, la prego, un ricordo per me, signorina »). Allora capì: il ricordo a uno sconosciuto era quanto, in figura di omaggio, la malasorte le concedeva. Raccolse da terra la bestiolina e docile acconsentì: la persuadeva il dolce tristissimo pensiero che almeno sul cartoncino della foto il piccolo maltese le apparterrebbe per sempre. Sedette stringendolo al petto e fissava gli alberi, le foglie dorate, i raggi di sole sulle cime dei pini con un'attenzione religiosa, come per non perdere nulla di un momento già memorabile. Non era soltanto il cucciolo che adesso le premeva; intuiva di esser giunta a un convegno irripetibile con se stessa: con la « signorina » che stava per firmare il suo futuro. Casualmente pareva essersi preparata a questo rito: non più colori delicati, ma un abito saviamente corretto, un tailleur scuro bordato di zagana, quasi una garanzia di serietà professionale. Un turbante di velluto rosso ciliegia le raccoglieva la gran massa dei capelli: la sfida che si era permessa. Accavallate le gambe, il busto un po' piegato in avanti, sostiene fra le mani guantate il bianco maltese che col suo musetto le nasconde il collo. Sul volto appannato dalla penombra già crepuscolare vaga un sorriso disincantato, un tantino ironico, che dice no alla giovinezza e le assottiglia le labbra senza scoprirle i denti. Negli occhi larghi, dalle orbite profonde si addensa un presagio notturno che nasconde l'assenza dello sguardo: a volte la tristezza riposa. « Un capolavoro » esclama il fotografo: ma lei, si alzò, disse che una foto bastava.

Le copie, fra cui questa, superstite, le furono consegnate quando tutto il peggio era avvenuto e sul puerile dolore del cucciolo non più suo era piombato il fulmine dell'estrema rinunzia, tante volte sfiorata, oggi fisicamente irrespirabile. Dopo l'ultima sfuggente stretta di mano (« sei una brava figliola, ti sposerai ») aveva voltato le spalle e via camminava tra la folla, per sempre allontanato. Lei non credeva di potersi muovere, ma ce la fece e si avviò lenta lenta, dalla parte opposta. Pianse, finalmente, senze ritegno né vergogna, così, per la strada, ridotta uno straccetto, e poi in una chiesa accesa di lampade natalizie non troppo indiscrete. Lì, in un angolo clemente, constatava inorridita che ventitré anni sono pochi, troppi ne debbono passare per raggiungere i limiti di una media vita umana: la vita che le toccherà vivere, sola, con dignità e coraggio, il suo unico riscatto. Non pregava di poter morire, ma che il tempo che le era assegnato passasse presto, per carità.

Lentamente, imparò ad attraversare l'onda dei giorni: come una malattia cronica, non mortale, la sfiducia condizionò il suo pensiero, i suoi studi, il suo lavoro. Sulla foto-cartolina che ogni tanto le capitava sott'occhio, fece un giorno una scoperta: to', quella melanconica damigella era davvero una bella ragazza, ma non era questo che contava, in quella immagine si configurava il modello della eterna « signorina », supplente al liceo, più tardi titolare di una cattedra, ma sempre definita da quel diminutivo fra pietoso e carezzevole, persino un po' buffo, col crescere dell'età: e lei, anche allora, ci avrebbe testardamente tenuto a questa etichetta con cui la società la segnava, senza più nome né cognome. I ricordi, custoditi in segreto — guai al collega sentimentale che vi accennasse — la mantengono in uno stato di armata adolescenza.

A volte, capitando in anticipo sull'orario nell'aula ancor vuota, appoggia la fronte alla vetrata: la strada del liceo sbocca nella piazza dove un tempo alloggiava Colui che si proibisce di nominare: e arrossendo le viene in mente l'unico giorno che entrò in quella stanza d'affitto, lei era vestita di bianco e di azzurro, lui era nervoso e disse: « mi dài soggezione ». Nel poco spazio di quella camera in disordine e in una mezz'ora di costosa disinvoltura era nato e morto il futuro che le spettava. « Buongiorno, signorina » saluta un giuggiolone di diciott'anni, il primo dei trenta liceali che stanno entrando in classe. Oggi Petrarca, domani Tacito, i suoi doveri. Non muore per mancanza d'amore chi per anni si è contentato di briciole pagate a caro prezzo;

ma questa privazione porta a una terribile pace. Fieramente, prendendosi in giro, la signorina partecipa a qualche ballo, una riprova che certi pericoli non esistono per lei. E difatti, ballando mai guarda il suo partner, non dice una parola, ma il ritmo le piace, preferirebbe danzare sola inventando passi e figure. Ha fama di superba, lei spiega che è soltanto timida ma sa bene che la sua timidezza è insofferenza della frase banale, del complimento goffo. Spesso sogna di esser costretta a sposare qualcuno, non sa chi, si vede all'altare e un no che non arriva a scoppiare le stringe la gola: allora si sveglia di soprassalto e respira con delizia la sicurezza della sua libertà. A chi le nomina un presunto innamorato, risponde sdegnata negando: come oserebbe, costui, prendere il posto di Chi l'ha rifiutata? Tale, pressappoco, la ragione del suo sdegno. A cuore chiuso, un tantino riottoso ammette con fastidio di essere attraente e si incupisce quando una scintilla di vanità la insidia suo malgrado. Lei non è di quelle che accettano il matrimonio borghese che ogni tanto le propongono: un così buon ragazzo, talmente innamorato. Sui suoi capelli di bronzo chiaro una parola è il suo diadema: « la signorina », guai a chi glielo tocca. Intanto si allena a una severa maturità, basta con gli anonimi omaggi floreali, con i bigliettini sciocchi nascosti fra le pagine del libro prestato: fra poco sarà una rispettabile zitella, alla maniera antica. Viaggia sola, va sola a teatro, vincendo ignobili pauracce quando, rincasando, si accorge di essere seguita. Non ha amiche.

Come prevedere che, invece, quella che è da tutti chiamata « vita », doveva ancora per lei incominiciare? Che il destino si sarebbe rovesciato scoppiandole in mano, la mano stretta da quella dell'indimenticabile Amico? La felicità è terribile, ti lascia nuda, indifesa, anonima. La « signorina » si allontanava, sciogliendosi nell'aria di un mattino di Pasqua, fra le colonne del Foro Romano, disintegrata nel sole e nel suono delle campane. Nessuno dei due ha spiegato, recriminato: la naturalezza del nuovo incontro garantisce una perfetta consonanza che anni di ambiguità — oh, così futili — non hanno mai corroso. Più giovane a venticinque che a diciott'anni, la ragazza, già così avida della propria infelicità, non ha lasciato traccia né contorni a questa che con un largo sorriso dai denti brillanti, esala da tutti i pori un fermo estatico stupore. Forse l'Amico le ha detto: come sei bella, ma lei non ci ha badato, non esiste più immagine di sé con cui abbia voglia di confrontarsi, ora che le offrono (ma lei ne ha un po' paura) un nome nuovo, una nuova situazione, strumenti che non sa usare. Sul suo orizzonte, tutto è troppo « pronto », troppo disegnato in anticipo, non è facile avvezzarcisi: essere una « giovane signora » la imbarazza, se ne vergogna, le sembra di non aver più parole né azioni sue e che il suo gioioso trionfo nasconda un laccio che talvolta la immobilizza nell'incanto di vivere nella casa dell'Amato, sedere alla sua mensa, sicura che ogni sera, presto o tardi, ascolterà con delizia girare la chiave nella toppa e i suoi passi che si avvicinano. Una sconfinata dolcezza la soffoca, le chiude gli occhi, le orecchie: la sua volontà è in pezzi. La passività è pericolosa: come un animaletto sazio e festoso avverte l'insidia dei ritagli di tempo libero, aperto al cappriccio. Che gli atti dell'amore, una volta spinosi e sconvolgenti siano, dall'oggi al domani non solo approvati ma quasi imposti da un nuovo codice, la turba. Dunque qualche cosa è cambiato: in meglio o in peggio? In meglio, in meglio si affretta a concludere, non senza qualche istintiva esitazione: in realtà il riconoscimento di certi diritti le pare una sgradevole mistificazione.

Disoccupata, si butta al lavoro subalterno ai compiti di segretaria: un ripiego sbagliato perché l'ordine, la precisione, la ricerca paziente non convengono alla sua natura. Il marito — ma sì! il marito — ride bonario, corregge le sviste e lei riconoscendo la sua dappochezza, odiandosi, si tira da parte, propone aiuti più elementari, battere a macchina, compilare schede. Cosa importa? Anche nascosta in un cantuccio sarebbe contenta. È bello che tutti i giorni siano uguali e che abbandonandosi al loro scorrere non sia necessario usare il cervello. Non che il cervello possa fermarsi: ma gira a vuoto o macinando frivolezze, bizzarrie, piccole impuntature. La volontà oscilla, pendula come una scimmietta nel bosco, il grande avvenimento è decidere se tagliarsi o no i lunghi capelli, una delle sue bellezze. Un salto nel buio è rimettersi allo studio del piano: mica male, approva, sorpreso, il generoso Ascoltatore. A un tratto la nube nera, la peggiore minaccia: presto o tardi egli si stancherà di una compagna senza interessi, senza problemi: troppo docile, sempre felice, uno sciocco gattino che gli ruzza fra i piedi.

Inutile illudersi, la felicità ha spento la sua intelligenza, l'ha confinata al ruolo di una furba accaparratrice. La « signorina » tradita si vendica: impossibile ritrovare l'antica solitudine, l'inziativa personale, il gusto delle difficoltà e un'ambizione tutta volta a dimostrare un valore misconosciuto. Chi sono, ormai? Una moglie che non discute, attenta al lampo di uno sguardo aquilino, agli umori di una suscettibile generosità. Non sa più dire « mi piace », « non mi piace », si crogiola nella rinunzia a decidere: ha persino disimparato a scegliere, i vestiti le cadono addosso come per magia, gli improvvisi viaggi la transformano in una piccola valigia utile al viaggiatore. Lui sa ciò che val la pena di guardare, sotto la sua mano il mondo si apre, non c'è che ascoltare e applaudire. Così passano la Francia, l'Inghilterra, l'Olanda, la cupa Germania. Ma a un tratto, inatteso, uno scatto: no, la giovane signora non andrà a Berlino, « questo mi basta » disse a Monaco, uscendo dalla Alte Pinakothek e si imbarcò sola per il Brennero. Una notte travagliata, desolazione e rimorsi. A Verona nel fresco sole, l'ombra della « signorina » ricomparve davanti alle porte di San Zeno[3] e al Pisanello:[4] pallida, trista, come rarefatta.

Fu un amaro viaggio: la sensazione di aver tradito qualcosa di prezioso la tormentava, ma la temporanea solitudine le permise di recuperare quel tanto di chiarezza che la felicità le aveva intorbidato. « Chi si ferma è perduto » ha detto uno sciocco: in fondo questo è il suo caso. Continuando avrebbe potuto pascersi d'illusioni, ora sa che i problemi da affrontare erano risolti in partenza: prendere o lasciare. Dunque mi sono ingannata, ho sbagliato strada. Ma qual era la mia strada? Un tuffo nell'infanzia, nell'adolescenza: e lo saprebbe. Ma non vuol rischiare, constata soltanto che se l'amore le è ormai indispensabile, esso non le è sufficiente e, insomma non la giustifica. Bando ai sogni logorati dal dubbio, eccitati da piccoli successi e talvolta dalla certezza dello scopo raggiunto: queste ambizioni non sono più per lei. Ma almeno una occupazione autonoma, da lei inventata, che la salverebbe dalla disistima di sé, dalla pigrizia: questo

---

[3]San Zeno Maggiore: chiesa romanzesca costruita nel quinto secolo e ricostruita dal dodicesimo al tredicesimo secolo.

[4]Antonio Pisano (c.1395–1455). Pittore e medaglista italiano. Il suo affescho si può ammirare nella chiesa di San Fermo a Verona.

pensava mentre il treno la riportava verso casa, inerme e vagamente irritata dagli sguardi che si posavano su di lei, ormai l'esperienza di una « bella donna », purtroppo. Un lavoro, un lavoro. Il più modesto, il più umile purché non casalingo, non legato alla condizione di chi può fare a meno di provvedere a se stesso perché altri « lo mantiene ». « Una mantenuta »: questa definizione banalmente demagogica, oggi, ahimè, le calzava come un guanto.

Riprendendo la vita normale l'idea coatta del lavoro a tutti i costi l'obbligò a fingere: e non era neppure facile perché la soggezione amorosa colmava la maggior parte del suo orizzonte: l'animaletto sazio e festoso ricompariva. Ma ogni giorno, l'ora X scattava. In una sospensione dolorosa, passava in rassegna le sue possibilità. Scartate con asprezza e dispetto quelle di ordine intellettuale, si chiedeva se non le convenisse umiliarsi applicandosi a un qualche lavoro manuale da cui tante donne ricavano da vivere. Di cucito, di recamo inutile parlare, lei ne era del tutto incapace, ma, da ragazzina aveva imparato a lavorare a maglia. Confezionare giubbetti da neonato, scarpine, sciarpe, scialli, non le sarebbe dispiaciuto, restava però il problema di come esitarli. Girellando oziosamente per certe viuzze popolari del centro, aveva notato una botteghina di merciaia che esponeva appunto di quegli indumenti. Più volte ci passò davanti e non senza rossore si propose di offrire alla merciaia un primo lavoretto. Comprò lana rosa e celeste e si chiuse in camera con ferri e gomitoli. Sferruzzava con accanimento timorosa che qualcuno la sorprendesse e potesse pensare... Infatti la domestica vedendola occupata in quel così insolito lavoro, aveva sorriso, ammiccando: evidentemente la credeva in attesa di un bambino. Era, lo capiva bene, una supposizione legittima e per nulla indiscreta, eppure, anche espressa da quella semplice ragazza la avvampò di dispetto. Fingere non volle e recisamente negò, a viso duro.

Il giubbetto fu terminato alla svelta e le parve un capolavoro, ma al momento di avvolgerlo nella carta velina, le cadde il cuore e sentì di aver perso l'ultima briciola di se stessa: il suo passato d'intellettuale schifiltosa le scottava la fronte e la condannava a un meschino sotterfugio, pagato a usura. Inventando che il lavoretto era opera di una povera giovane bisognosa, ne propose la vendita alla merciaia, una donnetta agra che, dopo averla squadrata, lo rifiutò come avrebbe rifiutato l'elemosina a un mendicante. Uscita dalla botteguccia, ad altro non pensava che a liberarsi dall'involto senza dar nell'occhio, quasi lo avesse rubato. Il tentativo di lasciarlo scivolare a terra non ebbe successo, un ragazzotto lo raccolse e glielo porse con un sorriso, la carta velina si era strappata lasciando intravedere il rosa delicato della lana. Alla fine il banco di una chiesa deserta risolse il problema, ma come l'atto fu compiuto, uno struggimento sottile la prese, parendole di aver davvero abbandonato un infante. L'ipotesi di una sua maternità mai l'aveva sfiorata fin dai tempi che, bambina, si dichiarava zia, non mamma delle sue bambole. Mai le era venuto in mente di discutere col marito la liceità di non procreare: intuiva che la paternità avrebbe disturbato il lavoro di lui, e questo sarebbe bastato a far tacere i suoi scrupoli, se mai ne avesse avuti. Ma non ne aveva, le piacevano i bambini, ma provava per loro una specie di rispettoso disinteresse.

Adesso, smaltita la frenesia del lavoro manuale, si lasciò andare a quella che le pareva la perdita definitiva della propria personalità: una perdita irrilevante, d'altronde, giacché ogni giorno la fulminea genialità del Compagno l'arricchiva e, insieme, la cancellava. Per diletto e, in un certo senso, per un patetico gusto celebrativo, si rimise a visitare musei e chiese illustri, a frequentare biblioteche dove, da ragazza, aveva trascorse intere giornate di letture remote, di ricerche che senza essere sistematiche, l'avevano inebriata. Al piacere rinnovato di quegli incontri si univa adesso il desiderio di prestare un segreto omaggio al grande studioso di cui portava il nome. Scrutando antichi testi e ritrovandovi talvolta i segni — a matita, sul margine — del suo lavoro di studente, stupiva di certe sue nuove interpretazioni. Alzando gli occhi dalla pagina si perdeva evocando quasi otticamente immagini di monaci astuti, di guerrieri bestiali, di città saccheggiate, di dense foreste intatte. Gli storici, i poeti della bassa latinità, i ceffi dei vandali, degli unni, l'affascinavano. A malincuore si riscuoteva riconoscendo che quelle lunghe letture non le servivano a nulla che non fosse favola, una favola che a nessuno avrebbe raccontata.

Sebbene molto restio alle relazioni di pura convenienza, alla lunga il marito l'aveva introdotta nella società di artisti, scrittori, poeti: lì fu, una volta per tutte, la graziosa signora X, piuttosto scostante. Fra quegli illustri si guardava bene dal rammentare la sua giovinezza laboriosa. Di che, infatti, avrebbe potuto vantarsi? Non certo del suo curriculum universitario, delle saltuarie supplenze nei licei: e meno che meno dei pochi articoli stampati su riviste accademiche. Le mogli che incontrava erano ragazze vivaci, con qualche cognizione di letture, di pitture, soprattutto di musica: nessuna aveva lavorato, ma conoscevano un sacco di gente e avevano la conversazione facile. Non l'avevano in simpatia, quelle donne, ma le apparivano così seducenti e ardite che, quasi a difesa, si applicò a migliorare il proprio aspetto con un lieve trucco, tanto da non scomparire fra quelle bellezze. Che suo marito potesse invaghirsi di una donna più attraente, più « interessante » di lei era possible e anche probabile: se ciò fosse avvenuto non le rimaneva che rassegnarsi senza pensare al futuro, la gelosia è un sentimento di lusso, solo chi è stato adorato può permetterselo. Le sue gelosie erano fulminee, taciturne e brevi: da ragazza s'era tormentata a proposito di una compagna di corso che a lei pareva un prodigio di grazia. A quel tempo, era certa che il suo idolo ne era preso, e gli dava ragione, in un certo senso l'amava anche lei, per procura. Mai avrebbe osato confrontarsi con quel volto di alabastro, quei capelli lisci di giaietto, quell'alta persona sottile dall'andatura ondulante. Ma io sono più intelligente, si consolava, straziata. Il pericolo era passato, forse non era mai esistito, ma ora prevedendo che un giorno o l'altro qualcosa di più grave accaduto, tentava di rassicurarsi studiando nel contegno degli uomini gli effetti della propria avvenenza. Incapace di civettare, blandire, bamboleggiare, si irritava, ironica, pungente. Pure, a volte le capitava di immaginarsi « servita » da un melanconico cavaliere, rispettoso, devoto. I crediti del suo difficile e avvilito amor giovanile non le davano forse diritto a qualche dolcezza? Non era giusto che avendo tanto data senza ricevere, ricevesse ora senza dare?

No, non era giusto, si sentiva colpevole e si deplorava. Per la verità i veri tradimenti della signora X si limitavano a qualche lacrima per la frase di un'antica sonata (l'appello di un morto di duecent'anni fa) o a un brivido per il ritornello di una canzone spagnola. Poi, spenta l'ultima nota, si accorgeva che il suo amore di sempre, struggente e quotidiano ingigantiva, assorbendo ogni forma di sentimento: di figlia, di madre, di sorella, di eterna innamorata e con radici sempre più intricate e profonde. Ne traboccava a tal punto che osò chiedere quel che non aveva mai chiesto: « mi vuoi bene? », e si stringeva al caro petto, se ne appropriava, insensibile ormai al timore di essergli importuna. La sua conquista era divenuta solida come una roccia, i dubbi, i rimpianti ci scivolavano sopra e scomparivano. « Siamo nati insieme », si esaltava, l'orecchio poggiato sul cuore di lui, ogni battito un rapimento, nel cavo della mano il suo omero così delicato quasi infantile.

Vivere giorno dopo giorno, in fondo non è difficile se non si è troppo esigenti: il mondo è un teatrino a cui partecipa anche chi sta dietro le quinte, alla peggio c'è sempre la risorsa di dormire e dormendo sognare, la signora X sogna moltissime cose, per esempio, quando ha l'emicrania, bellissime musiche. Cambiano le scene: lezioni di canto, partite di tennis, noiosissimi giochi d'impegno, il bridge, la canasta, con amiche occasionali che osservava incuriosita dimenticando le carte da pessima giocatrice che era. E cominciò a chiacchierare, lei, la silenziosa di un tempo. Senza rendersene conto quella sua nuova loquacità prendeva il ritmo del racconto gratuito: raccontava i suoi ricordi di bambina, le città dove aveva passata l'infanzia, e quanto aveva amato una sua incantevole zia, morta giovane. Parlando parlando, divagava, favoleggiava. Un po' stranite, le giocatrici finivano per trascurare picche e quadri e l'ascoltavano, calamitate. Sì, non c'eran dubbi, la signora X giocava malissimo ma raccontava bene: un rilievo non privo di malizia giacché era sottinteso che raccontava troppo.

Frecce spuntate. Una primavera incantevole spazzò via i tappetini verdi, le fiches, le carte, il whisky e le sigarette. A metà aprile il piccolo giardino casalingo si coprì di viola e di azzurro, le spine delle rose erano tenere come dentini di latte: dopo aver zappettato, annaffiato, giocato coi gattini dell'ultima covata si poteva sedere all'aperto, fra sole e ombra. Nulla mancava a quella scena idillica dove una protagonista, proiettata da vecchi romanzi alla George Sand,[5] prese a recitare diligentemente il ruolo della solitaria castellana, già vagheggiato nelle nebbie dei tredici anni. Nel boschetto dei lecci e degli eucaliptus una sdraio era pronta ad accoglierla insieme al libro ancora intonso, al quaderno degli appunti, alla stilografica. Si sedette, ma di leggere non aveva voglia, l'azalea fiorita le incatenava lo sguardo.

Fu a questo punto che il Caso operò: il quaderno, cadendole dal grembo in terra, s'era aperto, nitido, bianco, intatto, quasi in attesa di un segno. Nel raccoglierlo le scivolò di mano la penna che perse il cappuccio e lei non si curò di richiuderla, tenendola anzi per qualche istante so-

[5]Lo pseudonimo della scrittrice francese, Amadina Aurore Lucie Dupin (1804–76).

spesa sulla carta. Il sole meridiano occheggiando tra foglia e foglia ne disegnava i sinuosi contorni con tanta grazia che la mano, quasi da sé mossa, li seguì, tessendo un aereo arazzo di ombre perlacee. La pagina ne era tutta coperta, non restava che voltarla e rinunciare al gioco: un venticello brioso aveva scompigliato le fronde ma non inaridito l'inchiostro che ancora scorreva dalla sottile punta d'oro. La tentazione vinse, ai tenui ramaggi successero parole nomi: su cui una freccia invisibile faceva centro, per uno scopo non chiaro manovrato da una forza esterna ma benigna, il tenero inganno per cui i bambini piccoli sono costretti ad ubbidire. Parole, parole, parole: adesso la mano agile le rincorreva col ritmo dei soliti racconti alle « amiche » del bridge. Viveva la storia di un primo incontro con la morte, la morte di una vecchia signora amabile, coraggiosa, voltairriana, e sul foglio infittiva la grafia ispida, frettolosa con cui « la signorina » aveva un tempo annotato venerabili, difficili testi: del tutto diversa dai caratteri rotondi usati dalla signora X nei suoi frivoli biglietti di convenienza mondana.

Cominciava a piovere, una grossa goccia si allargava dilatando un « per sempre » sul punto di sbiadire. Fu cancellato e riscritto sull'asciutto e il quaderno fu chiuso.

Stringendolo sotto l'ascella insieme al libro, la signora si avviò verso casa, salì pian piano i gradini della veranda, insensibile alla pioggia che le bagnava i capelli e fasciava di un serico fruscio il silenzio immobile dell'aria, d'un tratto grigia. Anche l'interno della casa era silenzioso, tutti erano usciti, lo studio pareva disabitato, isolato nel tempo. Allora, come un giorno lontano, irripetibile, la signora appoggiò la fronte al vetro di una finestra e, a occhi chiusi, immaginò dietro le sue spalle il vuoto di un'aula polverosa. Il presente dileguava, unico rimaneva con lei e in lei il gesto or ora compiuto: tracciare parole non chiamate, non necessarie ma urgenti e quasi supplici, voci remote di immagini sul punto di dissolversi.

S'interrogava arrossendo: era dunque questo il segreto delle sue inquietudini: il pericoloso colloquio fra la carta e la penna che prometteva una seconda vita e per gli anni tardi — se pure verrebbero — l'unica vera pace. Sui vetri rigati di pioggia che il suo fiato appannava, alitava il volto un po' appassito della negletta « signorina ».

Essa perdonava, ma il prezzo del riscatto era alto.